CAUTERY

First published by Charco Press 2025
Charco Press Ltd., Office 59, 44-46 Morningside Road, Edinburgh
EH10 4BF

Copyright © Lucía Lijtmaer 2022
through MB Literary Agency

First published in Spanish as *Cauterio* (Barcelona: Anagrama)
English translation copyright © Maureen Shaughnessy 2025

The rights of Lucía Lijtmaer to be identified as the author of this work
and of Maureen Shaughnessy to be identified as the translator of this
work have been asserted by them in accordance with the
Copyright, Designs and Patents Act 1988.

A CIP catalogue record for this book is available from the British Library.

ISBN: 9781917260060
e-book: 9781917260077

www.charcopress.com

Edited by Fionn Petch
Cover design by Pablo Font
Typeset by Laura Jones-Rivera
Proofread by Fiona Mackintosh

This publication has been made possible with support from Acción
Cultural Española (AC/E).

2 4 6 8 10 9 7 5 3 1

Lucía Lijtmaer

CAUTERY

Translated by
Maureen Shaughnessy

CHARCO PRESS

CONTENTS

1. PLAÇA DE LES GLÒRIES (BEFORE)

For a long time, all I want to do is kill myself. I fantasise that I no longer exist, that I no longer have a body, and I find this idea inescapably peaceful. At first, I long for the tranquillity of a sea of barbiturates, like the sea after a storm, like a Caribbean beach with no swell. But, little by little, the fantasy becomes more sophisticated and a recurring image settles into my mind: the corners of my flat curve at the edges and turn into slides down which I slip, with nothing to grab onto. And then, as if everything were part of a sadistic experiment, I plunge into the abyss, toward the black tarpaper of my building's courtyard.

But I'm a coward and I don't kill myself.

I'm a coward. That's an important part of this story.

Over time, as I ride the number seven bus to work, the fantasy changes. One morning, at some tedious inter-section filled with weary-faced people whose backpacks are loaded down with Tupperware, I start to imagine the whole city flooding because of climate change.

The idea continues to take shape at the office where I work, a giant room housed inside a concrete block in Plaça de les Glòries. At the entrance some workers have mounted a huge backlit map of the Poblenou neighbourhood with the inscription 'District 22@: a district of the future'. From here, from this block of concrete that's identical inside and out, one of those architectural feats commissioned by the socialist party of the 1990s, I answer phone calls and think about The End.

While I envision straight lines between the Diagonal Mar shopping centre and Llacuna street and draft media plans to rationalise which ruinous buildings on Pallars street will be converted into design hubs with walls covered in cascades of ferns or into delivery logistics centres, my vision clouds with muddy water that invades my brain.

If the polar ice caps really are melting, Barcelona will be one of the first places to disappear, after Venice and Amsterdam. Then, being that it's on a ten to fifteen percent slope, the first to die will be the poor, the Pakistani taxi drivers from the Raval neighbourhood, the Filipina girls from the bakery on Sant Vicenç street, Señora Quimeta and her haberdashery, the expats living in Barceloneta – all of them, absolutely all of them: the Dutch, the French, the British and the Italians (no one will miss the Italians). The security guards, too, will float away, and the metro workers and the shopkeepers at the Santa Caterina market. To the south, the Llobregat river and all its reeds will become waterlogged. To the north, the Besòs river will overflow and the entire torrent will converge with the stretch of water between Sant Adrià and Cornellà, east and west, the stretch that will eradicate the airport and obliterate Castelldefels. In a random twist of fate, the Sakya Tashi Ling Buddhist temple of Garraf and the hippies from La Floresta will be spared. Only because the soil there is calcareous, so those houses won't collapse as easily. Fucking hippies.

The swampy water will cover everything. The last to go, no doubt, will be the posh ladies of Putxet, goddamned snobs. But they won't be spared. With their shiny pearls, their café con leche-coloured nail polish and their impeccable, indestructible lacquered hairdos, they'll float like gondolas down Balmes street – blue, dead, swollen – in the brown water that will drag everything, simply everything, along with it, down to the modernist Quadrat d'Or. It will take all the Pans & Company sandwich shops, the Liceu opera house, the tattoo artists on Tallers street. All the pseudo-authentic wine bars will flood. The ones that have old-looking furniture that's not actually antique. The ones with faux cement tile flooring, its sticky contact paper peeling back. The puddle-coloured, sewer-smelling water will rise above us all, even the rich and famous: Joan Gaspart, Núria Feliu, Andreu Buenafuente and Bibis Salisachs (who's already dead, but what does that matter?) The dead have been whispering to us for decades and we haven't cared to listen, I should know. The Maremagnum shopping centre will be reduced to a heap, swept away by the flood. So will the audiovisual communication department of the Pompeu Fabra University. And the Icària Yelmo matinée showings.

At night, I make lists of everything that will be destroyed by the rising sea levels. I can't stop. Colònia Güell, the National Theatre of Catalonia, the Billares bingo hall, the Hangar Arts Centre, all the Mercadona supermarkets, the Letamendi tax agency headquarters, Lord Byron bar on València street, the Theatre Institute, the Bruc barracks.

The Sutton nightclub will fall, the chocolate shops on Xuclà street will fall. The Golondrinas, those little wooden tourist boats that reek of fuel, will no longer be moored at the port. Instead, they'll turn up docked in some tree on Montjuic hill, where the water will also surprise two lovers getting it on in full swing, dying with their pants round their ankles.

It is with this image in my head, and this image alone that, on my way home from work, when I'm buying groceries, I ask for extra plastic bags. I'm so desperate for us all to drown that I leave the lights on at home and I don't recycle. If I knew how to drive I would tear down the Carretera de les Aigües. I would take off from the Ronda de Dalt beltway at 145 kilometres per hour, tank filled with highly polluting petrol. Something to scorch the flora, to choke the wild boars, to speed up the process. We're all going to poison ourselves together so why not accelerate this group ritual, let's give it our all, once more with feeling!

But I can't manage to pull it off. Instead, I move to Madrid. Which is not so different from dying after all.

I. DEBORAH UNDERGROUND

I don't know whether or not I'm alive.

I suspect that I'm not. The earth surrounding me is just dust, so different from the dark clay of my childhood. The soil on my forehead is salty, I don't understand why. And on my arms, between my legs, dirt that tastes of salt and sea. I can hardly open my eyes, I'm covered by earth on all sides. They say that salt cauterises, but over the years I've learned that it also corrodes and destroys everything it touches.

I can't be alive, all this weight on my shoulders, and yet I feel no pain. My lungs are empty, this soil is unfamiliar to me, I don't remember it. The pastures of my childhood were dewy, pale green, always thick with moisture. The woods, in contrast, were dark in winter. The air sliced through one's breath, a sharp knife scratching from within. There's no air inside me now, nor water – only time.

I'm definitely not alive because worms slither around, soft as Chinese silk, tickling my skin.

Chinese silk. The scent of exotic fruit. The memory of our first night together. No, not now. This rat-grey dirt is no place for our blood. Not now that I've been hollowed out, now that someone has removed my entrails and my body bears the entire weight of time and of this unfamiliar soil.

I should start with the afternoon he turned up at my house to ask for my hand, or perhaps even before that, back when we first met. It was three months earlier, at the stables. I wore my hair long, very long. I'd never cut it despite the fact that my mother insisted otherwise. I wouldn't let them cut it. It was tied back tightly in a thick bun that weighed me down. My skirt perfumed, my hands scrubbed clean with soap. All grown-up, twenty years old. My parents didn't let me go to dances, all I knew were the green fields, Sunday service, the cold stone church and the maps my father showed me in books. 'Look at the streets, Deborah. Do you see them?' I traced the city streets with my finger, they were copper-coloured rivers writhing like snakes, like knots in wood.

He entered the stables in search of the foreman, but found only the housekeeper and me, feeding the horses. It was November, we used to spend part of autumn and winter in the countryside, far from London. I missed the city terribly, but my father insisted on returning to the house where he was born in the season when wild mushrooms grow and Michaelmas daisies bloom, the month of chestnuts and deer hunting.

The man was tall, he had a blond beard and curious eyes. He asked permission from my companion to sit down with us on a bench outside the stables. What type of bridles do you use, miss? He enquired without asking my name, because he already knew it. He had small hands and dressed in clothes unlike the townsmen, and he wore a ring with a tiny stone, a stone I had never seen before that he called a 'sapphire'. We talked about the weather, the chestnuts, the horses. Their manes gleamed, my body boiled, my red, red blood. I felt my blood burst, splitting into tiny drops like molten metal, red and orange, like liquid crystal when it burns, and then my face flushed. 'Your face is the colour of apples,' he said, and he roared with laughter. And when the housekeeper got up for a moment he whispered a profanity into my ear, 'Are you the type of girl who runs fast and comes quickly, like the horses?' And I felt dizzy and shook my head. Then she came back and said, 'That's enough now, Henry. Let her be. The girl is from a good family. Go on home.'

Now, so many years later, I feel my unresponsive body, bearing such heavy weight on my head and shoulders. I suppose this means I've been buried vertically, with my arms in the form of a cross. That's why all the weight is on my head, my spine, right where the nape of my neck meets my back. All this dirt surrounding me, above and below, is made of some substance I cannot distinguish. Something stings, it's the salt. This earth is so hard it cuts my arms, my hands, my feet. The abrasions are barely the size of an ant, like when a sheet of paper nicks your finger. Although the weight should be excruciating, pressing on my neck and temples, I feel strong. I feel no pain, none at all. I grasp at a handful of dirt and clench it in my hand. Now I see. This soil is mixed with sand, a beach of pulverised molluscs. Up above, everything must be water and salt.

What am I doing here underground? If they buried me vertically it's because no one claimed my body. It's because I'm damned. And the worst part is, not only am I dead, but I was not saved. Oh Lord, I'm dead. I had faith in you and yet you have abandoned me. I crossed oceans for you, just to end up buried underground like a worm. I didn't even make it to purgatory. How could you do this to me? God Almighty, you took no pity on me. Your eyes were jewels that I adored despite it all, and yet I have been deserving of nothing. I was a good woman – this

I want to believe – and you have condemned me to the salty sand where nothing bears fruit, where nothing grows. Why? Why have you abandoned me so?

Then, suddenly, Anne Hutchinson's face appears before me, wan and haggard. Her loose hair, her pale hands, right here in the dirt, and I understand.

2. CALLE DEL CALVARIO (NOW)

It is here on this scorched plateau that my story begins. I find a flat on a street that, like every street in Madrid, has been named after something taken from a Castilian Catholic village. I think I'll be better off in Madrid. Yes, I hope so. I'm almost optimistic. Almost. Since my senses are numbed it takes me longer to understand the differences here, which are actually so plain to see.

For example, everyone is nice in Madrid. Especially in the afternoon. This is before I realise everyone is drunk in the afternoon. The doorman of my building, a Belarusian with slicked-down hair and a Prince of Wales suit, is the first to tip me off. In the morning he doesn't greet me, but by afternoon he's tremendously cheerful. He winks at me, tells me dirty jokes and lurches a bit. It takes longer than it should for me to grasp the situation because vodka doesn't leave any scent on his breath, the old fox.

It's the same story with the rest of the neighbourhood. The mornings are fresh, and everything seems sleepy until noon. Then they all wake up and stretch out, moaning about their hangovers. The waiters, the shopkeepers, the lady at the tobacco kiosk. Everything moves slowly, like a remote village. It's all so different from night time. It's not long before I realise that I've made a rookie mistake: I've rented a flat above a bar with a terrace. Manzanita blares from the speakers every night, and when the neighbours implore for some peace and quiet and the pub finally closes, car radios come alive with cumbia and reggaeton. Revelry is the city's first commandment and my street is its temple: a karaoke of drunks crooning until five o'clock in the morning.

A karaoke of drunks simmering at an incessantly feverish temperature. Nobody ever mentioned how hot it gets in Madrid, or at least I must have decided to ignore any warnings. I moved here in the middle of August, which means that I live in an oven that's always on. The asphalt is perpetually hot, even at night, and I can't sleep. I don't touch the moving boxes for weeks, unable to move a muscle. I buy plants at a sleek shop in the neighbourhood to cheer myself up, and they die on me in a heartbeat. Everything refuses to grow in Madrid. Everything is, or winds up, fried.

One day, in the lift, I strike up a conversation with the woman who lives upstairs. She's somewhat older than me, but she doesn't look it. She has dark hair, almond-shaped eyes and pale skin. I see a pleasant smile with large horsey teeth. Her lips are painted red and she's wearing a flowered dress. Her name is Sonia. I notice her firm thighs, delicate skin, the bags under her eyes. She's wearing gold earrings. With a whiny, weary voice she asks if the heat is keeping me up at night, too. I tell her that I can't sleep either. She invites me over for lemonade and I accept. I have nothing better to do.

Her flat is pretty, luminous. There are shelves made from wooden fruit crates, plants everywhere and books strewn around on the floor. I wonder if the plants are made of plastic. I wonder if she might be a witch and able to keep things alive by magic. She's hung tapestries on the walls – to 'block out the noise', she says.

Sonia serves me some lemonade and keeps talking. The shrill tone of her voice gets on my nerves, but maybe it's just been too long since I've interacted with anyone. I've become unaccustomed to the sound of someone else's voice in the same room.

'Do you live alone?' I ask, feigning interest.

'Yes.'

'Cool.' I look at the books stacked all around, on the shelves, on the floor, between the furniture. 'Do you work at the university?'

'Not exactly. Right now I'm just studying.'

She squirms in her chair. I notice a hint of concern in her answer.

I smile.

'I don't work,' I say to help her relax.

'Really? How's that?'

'I don't need to work.'

Sonia blinks very quickly several times in a row, like a hummingbird. Bzzz.

'What does your husband do?' she asks me.

'I'm not married.'

'Oh.'

Another bzzz.

Finally she understands what I'm trying to say. I'm trying to imply that I'm rich.

Too bad it's not true. The money I've got is only because of what I did. Because of what I let them do to me. And now I've got enough to last me a year without working. Even so, I enjoy watching the expression on her face when I insinuate this. Rich. I observe as her mind shifts gears. It's fun. Astonishment at first, followed by supressed envy, and when that emotion comes to an end it condenses into something invisible but penetrating, which settles in like a bad smell: everyone who thinks you're rich wants something from you. They want your money. Or at least they want *something*. And once they realise it, they feel embarrassed and somewhat guilty. As I now know, guilt is a despicable feeling that we all want to be relieved of. After experiencing this whole flood of emotions that occurs in just a few seconds, the other person starts to offer you things nonstop without realising it, to shake off that sensation that's making them feel so bad.

'Would you like to have dinner with me this week? I know a great Peruvian spot,' she says. 'My treat.'

See what I mean? It never fails.

That same night, from above the boiling pavement, from this new insomniac calvary, I'm illuminated by the computer screen. I spend hours online searching for something to appease me, and tonight I find it in the grooves of rivers and seas, in old maps, in the stories of those who have drowned before us. That's how, at six o'clock in the morning, after staying up all night, I come across the portrait of a woman who witnessed the drowning of a girl in 1642. It's been taken from her chronicles, transcribed into a blog online. Her portrait depicts a dour gaze and puckered lips. The title of the post is 'The Cautery Chronicles'. I'm struck by the composure in her writing as she relates how they pulled a dead baby from the river. I read her name, Deborah Moody, a puritan who took up exile in the North American colonies in the seventeenth century. I look at her face, like that of a piglet fattened for the slaughter, and her eyes bulging like two hard-boiled eggs. 'The first woman to found a settlement and design a town in the New World', says the forum on historical crimes.

I imagine her slicing a gash into the earth, like someone quartering an animal, someone who knows exactly what they're doing: the minimal effort, wholly efficient. A cross on the ground, X marks the spot, and a square in the middle. Voilá. With that her town was created. Now it's a lot more complicated, you can't go around drilling holes in the ground wherever you please. If only. If only that's how things worked, I would grab a drill to get myself out of here, I'd dig a tunnel and bury myself there, safe, at peace, no need to breathe.

The following night I have dinner with Sonia at a mediocre restaurant downtown and she tells me that she's an escort for construction companies. Cement plants, aluminium manufacturers. Gentlemen smoking cigars who seal big-money contracts with a blowjob under the table of a restaurant booth with a tablecloth skirting to the floor. In Plaça de les Glòries, I once heard talk about these types of meetings with members of the city council, but I thought they were urban legends. Legends of urbanism we used to call them at the office. Haha. But Sonia's secret now repulses me – not because of what she does, it's because she doesn't know me. I don't like the fact that she confided in me, and her secret adheres to me like a slimy jellyfish. After a week I decide to move to a flat where I don't have to speak to anyone. I find an office building in the Castellana district that has a couple of penthouses for rent. I don't want to have friends. I've had friends before. A lot of good that did me.

II. DEBORAH &
THE GREY TURTLE DOVE

The day that Anne Hutchinson died, right in the middle of the night, a grey turtle dove alighted at my window. I was awoken by its guttural sounds and I turned over in bed to try and sleep some more, but my skin was burning. Old age brings with it so much skin to lug around with you, like a bale of hay. Here's the truth: old age is feebleness. Sagging skin, loose teeth, bulging veins.

Just before sunrise I gave in and got up and made myself a cup of black tea in the kitchen. The maid was still asleep and there was no need to wake her: it was going to be a long day. So many years had passed and still I missed the insipid herbal infusions of my childhood. There were only strong smells and flavours in the colonies, things to kill the pain and obliterate any subtle nuances.

The weight of my body reminded me of my mother when she said: you have hips made to bear children, wide and strong. That was the only nice thing she ever said about my body. She always insisted I wear clothes that chafed my skin, to make it look smaller, bust too big, hips too wide, everything too large. But that day at the stables I noticed him discerning my body beneath my dress, imagining it with nothing on top, and I knew that I would have to give birth to his children. So I concentrated all my blood down there, the blood that tastes of copper but which is made of molten iron, and I looked him in the eye and he held my gaze.

Will you come to tea one day? I blurted when I could take it no more, and the housekeeper whispered, 'Shush girl, a woman mustn't speak up or offer invitations, shush now', but he said, 'Yes, yes, I'll come.' That night, so far in the past, I thought of his hands, and of the little stone ring, dark blue like the eyes of the peacocks rumoured to live at the king's palace. I thought of his fingers caressing that precious stone until I fell asleep.

We were married three months later, on a day at the end of February, in that month that is nothing but an extension of the dark night.

I insisted on wearing a pearl grey dress which my mother detested, with tulle sleeves down to the wrists. The fittings with the dressmaker took a month. He and I only saw each other twice from the time we met until we were wed, always in the company of others. It was a marriage in haste, but which no one was going to protest. I knew my father was relieved to marry me off, finally.

I remember nothing of the ceremony, only that it was quite cold and rainy, and the grey of the sky was much darker than that of my dress. And as we left the church he told me I looked like a dove from the countryside in that grey dress, the tulle, my perfumed gloves embroidered in silver – the only extravagance I had allowed myself. 'You're like a dove to hunt down. Bang, bang! I'll pump you full of lead,' he said, roaring with laughter.

When I arrived at my new house: large, dark and filled with objects – so different from my own – I touched them one by one, and told myself: all this is mine. These curtains, this furniture, even the brooms. All mine. The maids who lowered their heads as I walked by couldn't help but raise their eyes and stare at me. I saw it all in their gaze, especially the prettier ones. That look that meant: why would a man such as he choose a woman so lacking in substance. I gripped my husband's arm tightly to steady myself amongst all those rooms, all those servants and everything so new. Once it was over, at night, in bed, I told him: 'They all think you married me for my money.' And he didn't respond, he just pried my legs open with his knee.

The grey of my dress, I think. The grey sky from my first flush of youth, so distant, so many years ago. It was exactly the same grey of the turtle dove perched on my window announcing to me that Anne was going to die, forty years after my wedding night.

3. PASEO DE LA CASTELLANA, 11
(NOW)

I wasn't always like this.

Wasn't always this crazy, is what I mean.

I wasn't always this much of a coward.

I open a Coca-Cola Zero, swallow a Xanax and turn the A/C on low. The bubbles make me feel bloated, but they trick my stomach too. I've stopped eating. I turn down Sonia's invitations for an entire week. I look at myself in the mirror. If the old me could see myself now she'd be proud. I've finally become slender, now that it no longer matters. So many years of obsessively measuring my hips, those mounds of belly fat, one on top of the other. How I would have ripped them out if I could. The tons of vomit, the laxatives, the punishment. All that time beating myself up, woefully groaning as if I were a little puppy dog. Stupid girl. All it took was losing my appetite. If I were really here, if my girlfriends were here with me, we would delight together in affirming how, day after day, the contours of my thighs diminish, how my collarbone sharpens, how I lose muscle mass. My friends would surely applaud me, but they aren't here, I lost them a while ago.

Nervous system depressants are like a time bomb. The neck slackens, I can feel my brain acquiring the consistency of a sea sponge. It fills with much-needed holes.

From behind the tinted windows of my flat I watch the office workers who, clad in suits, pause for a coffee break in front of the vestibule to my building. It's mid-morning. A man in his thirties with a cobalt blue tie and sideburns somewhat longer than normal – he must be the rebel at the insurance company where he works – flirts with a long-haired blonde in a cream-colored dress. I imagine her nails are painted in a French manicure to match the dress. Tanned feet, white teeth. Japanese hair straightening. I daydream. She lives in Chamberí, but she's from Valladolid – where she goes back to visit her lifelong boyfriend every two weeks, driving a Renault Twingo. Sideburns is from the outskirts of Madrid, and his personality consists of listening to Vetusta Morla. He'll want to do it up the ass on their first date, which he'll feel guilty about so he'll settle for a hand job. After three rendezvous he'll get what he's after, she'll let him, she won't go back to Valladolid that weekend or the following one, using work as an excuse. By then she'll have made it official with the new guy and he won't be able to admit that what he really wants is for her to pretend like a twelve-year-old boy who loves semen.

I wasn't always like this.

There was a time when I didn't wake up at quarter to five in the morning – now I do, it never fails – to flick through catalogues of Anthropologie rugs. I didn't used to think, day after day, that I was going to die. Now I check my skin obsessively. I search for symptoms of Kaposi's sarcoma. I take my temperature. I notice how my gums are receding due to a lack of vitamins. When

I feel like I should be doing something, I buy the same Caesar salad at the supermarket – my only outing – and wolf it down sitting on a bench where it's forty degrees Celsius in the shade, before returning home to lie down again on the sofa. Blisters appear on my tongue from the excess of salt, from the dehydration. I buy my clothes online, I accumulate plastic bags and fall into the black hole of chemical slumber.

I suppose there was a time when it could have been said I was happy. I can prove it by the digital footprint I left online, the same transparent trail made by a slug. I don't remember anything, but it seems like I had a normal job, a schedule. I went out to eat, I had friends, I got haircuts. I had sound viewpoints about domestic and international politics. I read books, I accumulated copies of the *New Yorker*.

No memories and my brain is filled with holes, but there's a constant refrain in my head about that whole time period: my friends and I once heard about a girl who'd gone crazy for real. To us, going crazy and being humiliated seemed like the worst thing in the world. 'She's infatuated with a married man', my friend told us, 'and now she goes around making a fool of herself everywhere. She turns up at his work and cries. She cries to anyone who will listen. The guy couldn't care less about her. He was just killing time, then he got bored.'

Kill some time, rip it to shreds, cook it up on the grill with some butter and sage, I think. Serve it up on a plate and pair it with a good Bordeaux. That's what he did. Good for him. All the while that girl I'd never met was bawling in public at every concert, every dinner party, every self-respecting social function. There she was, refusing to move on, her mascara running, her hands shaking, wearing an acrylic dress and tights with runs in them.

And you know what? I was so happy that I laughed at her. I was so happy, I was so untroubled, that I locked arms with you and told you the whole story on our way home.

Oh, right. You.

We should talk about you, shouldn't we? Yes, we should.

III. DEBORAH & THE CAUTERY

In my memory, the healer has white eyes the colour of milk, the same white as the eyes of the Africans who wander around the colony, terrified, their surroundings so unfamiliar to them. 'A port is like a gaping mouth, it can be filled with the most enchanting wonders, but also with infection,' Anne Hutchinson used to say, always preoccupied by saving, cleaning, disinfecting everything she saw. So easily fooled, without actually taking a look around her.

Anne sympathised with the Africans drifting around the port and losing their minds, so far from home. We watched as they trudged from here to there asking for money, for food, a roof over their head. Anne Hutchinson, with her pale hands gnarled from hard labour, with her authentic smile, her high-pitched and intelligent voice, always eager. I, in contrast, looked at their youthful faces and was scared of them. I'd grown old. It wasn't their appearance that left me unnerved. After all, there are slaves throughout the New World. I wasn't a prig. I didn't feel the need to save them, like Anne, who brought them into her home, sitting them side by side with her children, and tried to educate them on the love of God and a righteous life. I knew that moving from one world to another can drive you crazy, much crazier than anything else. I looked at the veil covering the eyes of the slaves as they disembarked in America, like the film that forms on milk once it's been boiled: a troublesome membrane covering everything. Smooth as velvet to the touch, but I would have burned my hand every time, like when I was a girl. I always tried to retrieve that greasy film from the saucepan. It tastes like nothing and slips through one's fingers. Alas, so much time had passed since my childhood.

Many years ago, before I grew old, the healer looks at me with those same milky eyes and spreads my palms open wide. We're in her cabin, which smells of leather and the fur of some animal. Behind us, the coals in the fireplace and two dishes of stew. She offered it up when I arrived but I cannot eat, I'm too nervous. I shouldn't have come. I've escaped from under the eyes of the housekeeper to make my way here. You'll get help there, but don't tell a soul, my older cousin had said when, desperately, I confessed my distress, how I've been unable to sleep. And that is why I am here with the healer, who holds my palms between her hands, which are hot and firm. She's plump and affable, and this surprises me. I expected her to be different, I suppose, with inquisitive eyes. Not a maternal and warm woman. She laughs and I feel reassured, like I could tell her anything, everything. She strokes my open palms and then presses the base of my two thumbs against her own. I feel a stab of pain and she smiles.

'You're tense and your pulse is erratic. Are you having trouble sleeping?'

I nod.

'Your nerves are shot, girl.'

She sighs and tells me to sit in the rocking chair and close my eyes with my arms outstretched in a cross.

When I do, I hear the creaking wood and her breath upon me. Right away, she begins to rub my limbs with her hands, as if trying to warm them up. She does this for an indefinite period of time, until my whole body responds and the cold subsides, until I've become used to the smell of her house.

I hear the fire crackling and the scuff of a chair as she sits down. She clears her throat.

'Open your eyes and tell me why you came.'

Her round face, slanted eyes and wide smile are once again before me. I look at her crooked and somewhat grey teeth, her pleasant face, covered in freckles. She looks like a child, not a healer, I think.

'I'm going to be married.'

'As if I didn't know. The whole county knows. You're marrying Moody, the trader. A man who will have a political career, not bad. You won't be poor, if that's what's worrying you. He's well connected.'

'No.'

'What exactly do you want to know. Whether you'll have children?'

'No. I want to know whether or not I should get married.'

'That's not a question. Every woman should get married. That's not why you're here.'

I don't answer. The woman takes my hands between hers once more and rubs. She knows they've gone cold again, despite the fire.

'Lie down,' she says, pointing to a bed piled with animal furs. It looks soft and comfortable.

The healer lights a stick of wood that gives off a very strong smell and I hear the tinkling of little bells. I open one eye to see that she's tracing my body with the stick, I believe it's sandalwood, not more than a few centimetres from my skin.

'Close your eyes or it won't work! Listen up. You're travelling downriver on a boat,' she says, 'the river is long. There are rapids, there are rocks. What do you see?'

'I see my family on the shore. My parents. They see me but cannot reach me.'

'And what else.'

'There's someone next to me on the boat, but I can't make out their face.'

'That doesn't matter. You'll have time to discover their face.'

'Is it my husband?'

'It doesn't matter, don't ask questions. What else do you see?'

'The boat is rocking. The person with me is shaking it. I think we're going to fall out. And the water's so cold! I don't want to fall in.'

'You won't, hold on tight.'

'I see something else… I don't quite know what it is… a grey stone. It's polished, breathtaking, with glints of colour.'

'A diamond?'

'No. No, it's a grey stone, but one side has vivid colours: greens, blues, violets. They shine in the dark. I've never seen anything like it. It's so beautiful.'

'What's it called? Can you name it?'

'I don't know the word for something like this. I've never seen anything like it.'

'Try to find the word.'

I feel a name escaping from my mouth like a soap bubble, like an egg emerging from a hen, slippery. An enormous round presence that wasn't here a minute ago. Opal.

'It's an opal,' I say.

'That word doesn't exist, Deborah.'

'I know that's what it's called. The stone I see is called opal.'

When I open my eyes the healer is squinting at me with her milky eyes. She's grown serious and is no longer smiling. She goes to a cupboard and brings back a bottle and two glasses. She pours and says firmly:

'Drink.'

I do, feeling the fiery liquor burn its way down my throat.

'It's been a long time since I've witnessed anything like this. It takes thousands of years to create a mineral, a few hundred to be discovered and mere seconds to be named. You've found something that has yet to be discovered, but which was already there, buried and waiting for you. You've given it a name. You think that you came here today to find out whether your future husband loves you, but God actually brought you here because your mission is much more important, even though you're nothing but a simple woman. Forget about love, that's not what marks your destiny. None of the men in your life will have much importance. You've come for me to tell you your fate, and this is what I see: you will make two journeys and there will be much water along the way. Your crossing over will lead you to discover that the men in your life are dull but capable. They will all betray you. You will give them all of your power and they will give you nothing in exchange. Knowing what I've just told you will change nothing. That will be your downfall, and although you know it, you will not be able to alter your destiny. There will be gold and there will be blood. But, most importantly, you will encounter an angel with blond hair. How you act in its presence will determine your future. Remember the angel, above all else.'

The woman rummages inside a bag.

'Allow me to give you something to protect yourself.'

From a leather bag she removes a long, silver instrument, curved at one end and with a wooden handle.

'This is a cautery. Take a look. When you heat it up in the fire it changes colour. It can be ashen, cherry red, crimson, and its purpose is to cure. It can isolate infections by burning. It will serve to purify that which you must save. It is important for you to stay healthy. You are young, but still have a long journey ahead.'

My hands and feet have gone numb, and the healer instructs me to stand up. She walks me to the door of her cabin, and as I place the silver object in my wicker basket she says:

'Do not forget, gather your strength now. You will live far from here, Deborah, very far. You will go to places that have not yet been named and which, therefore, seem not to exist, like the stone you saw. But something unprecedented will happen to you: you will make the crossing twice. You will live here and somewhere else by the sea. Do not forget that. For you, the journey will be more important than your fate. Remember the journey and its stones. And the angel, more than anything else, the angel and its lovely hair. That angel will determine everything.'

4. CARRER DE L'ALMIRALL
BARCELÓ (BEFORE)

The real inception of our tale, the one that really counts, takes place at a wine bar – the bar's name doesn't matter – where three women in their thirties are slowly getting drunk. It's on one of the narrowest streets in Barceloneta, one where the sun never shines.

The setting is important for this story. The wood is polished, the floors are mosaic-tiled, the bar is marble. The rediscovery of old bars serving wine straight from the barrel has just experienced a boom in Barcelona, all those lacquered oak barrels, hand-scribbled with the per-litre price of sweet wine. They're called bodegas, but they're actually just overpriced bars where people can drink a glass of draft beer that's considered to be well-poured. Or some run-of-the-mill wine and tinned mussels that cost their weight in gold, and everyone feels 'authentic and local'. Over time I've learned that 'authentic and local' is just another way of saying 'dirty and sans-Danish tourists and non-EU migrants'. When it comes to their bars, Barcelona natives are unscrupulously racist, *primer els de casa*: they look after their own first.

My two friends look at me, expectantly. We all know that it's my moment to shine. I contemplate their dilated pupils, how they behold me with their lips parted, waiting for me to start. I let the moment draw out. I pause and observe them. They're both wearing jeans and spring blouses, they smell good. On their wrists are bracelets from a trip they took together to Bolivia, and they share a llama tattoo inked one crazy night on that same trip. Tell us everything, they say as we munch on some mediocre sausage from Extremadura at eighteen euros a plate.

'I don't know, it was so strange.'

'Start from the beginning.'

'But you've both already heard it before.'

'When did you kiss?'

'At the third bar, I don't remember.'

'What do you mean you don't remember?'

'I don't know, I don't remember. Besides, what does it matter? That was two months ago. We've been together for two months.'

'He's your boyfriend!'

My friends screech with joy like two raucous birds, two parrots that have swooped into the tallest trees on the avenue, that is their exact laughter. People at the bar turn to look at us for a moment and I get a glimpse of us from the outside: three thirty-somethings shouting and drinking beer, one spring afternoon. My friends applaud, this is a party although I don't quite know what we're celebrating. They lean in conspiratorially around the table and ask for more details. They need to complete internal databases, do mental formulas and calculate square roots on the chances of our relationship. On the probability that this could actually work out. What could go wrong with this story?

They order more beers, gesturing to the waiter, and they demand more, more of everything. My spirits lift and I continue relating how we met, standing at the bar of a pub the three of us used to go to, on Botella street, in the Raval, and how I recognised him from a city council meeting, he was one of the few people there our age who didn't look like a bank clerk. 'I like his sideburns,' I say, and it sounds ludicrous. Summing up the person you like always sounds foolish, the concrete details end up seeming absurd. How to describe someone you like? It's as if you were talking about a piece of furniture, or a pair of shoes. I tell them how you looked at me from afar and said something to the waitress that I would later find out was 'I like that girl', and that you approached me to say hello, and there was rockabilly music playing, which I hate, but I feigned interest because of your sideburns, assuming you must like rockabilly. We talked about bands, about how boring city council meetings are, and I saw a glimmer somewhere on your face, an invitation that made me think *something* could be possible. Admiration, I think. You listened a lot, spoke little. You laughed at my jokes. I felt like something about me was important. Like at that instant, at that bar, we were starting something. Like they would have to hang a plaque, someday, about us being there. IT ALL STARTED HERE: WINTER OF 2012. One of those discreet, bronze commemorative plaques with engraved lettering, painted black.

But I don't mention that last part. I just murmur something about how you're a sociologist, how you work at City Hall, like me. How you like to cook.

The two parrots widen their eyes, their pupils dilate, and one asks what your surname is and, naturally, she's heard of it, because Barcelona is like that, everyone knows each other, and they say more, more, more, and they chew on the story and on the mojama tuna and I carry on: he told me that I'm the woman of his dreams. He says he wants children. And they howl with pleasure, and then they're no longer birds but suckling she-wolves, enraged and insatiable. Now I get it, I tell myself. This is the monogamy party. I had forgotten. Now I belong to this club. I haven't always been part of it. But it's better to belong here than not to. It gives purpose to everything. It's an infectious club, comfortable and monotonous, like a sedative.

They ask, 'When are you going to move in together? You shouldn't wait too long.' The one who knows him, because everyone knows each other in Barcelona, says, 'Have you seen his ex? No, the other one, the blonde. She can be pretty funny but she's crazy. Crazy for real – not like you, he'll be happy with *you*. You won't make him suffer.' The important part of all this, the three of us think but don't say out loud, is not to end up being a head case. And I remember the girl with runs in her tights, and I don't know why, but I envision her out in the rain, her hair drenched, as if she just emerged from a river, lost and sleepless. Suddenly I feel uneasy and I don't know why.

Before ordering another three beers and finally changing the subject, I take mental note of my homework: look up the pictures of his ex on social media, check whether she seems happy, whether she still lives far away, in another city, whether she's in a relationship, whether she ever gets in touch with him, whether she wants him back, this trophy I've just acquired in the form of a man. That's how I used to think, back then, in that bodega, when I still had a job, a schedule and a future; when I formed part of that labyrinth of greyish streets like a fungus growing on tree trunks; when I went out at night and had hangovers on Saturdays; when I still remembered names and faces and had a life; when I still had a functional life and not just these four glass walls in the vile summer heat.

Not like now when, day after day, I wake up and say to myself: 'I'm sick. Someone will find me out. My blood is sick, someone will punish me: nobody makes it out alive from all this.'

IV. DEBORAH & THE MERCURY

The calcified dirt on my forehead reminds me of my youth. The weight of the sand is like the weight of a man: constant, never yielding.

In all this time underground I have brooded over those first nights in my new house and the cold green mantle surrounding me. Rhododendrons, ivy, azaleas. I remember the first few months, how much I tried to make that house my own. There are several things a woman in my position is told, but no one ever shared them with me because my mother stopped talking to my father and me early on. Nothing beyond the indispensable words exchanged around the table. When my breasts grew she looked at my hips with disgust, murmured that I was 'as wide as a cow' and shut herself away with the Scriptures. She left me under the care of the maids, who didn't have the authority to help me understand anything about myself, the heir, the only child.

One of the things no one explained to me is how one organises a house. How unprepared my mother left me to face the world! She thrust me at a man like someone tossing clothes in the laundry basket, without much consideration, and withdrew back into her silence and her prayers. Much later, I understood that running a household is like running a ship. There's always work to be done, orders to give, surfaces to clean, everything must be anticipated. There is no rest, least of all a good night's sleep. Orders must be given to hang out the rugs, smooth down the sheets, change the mattresses. Decisions made on what to do with the geese, the cows and the pigs, when to serve which dishes to which dinner guests. That's right, the dinner guests. My husband hosted sumptuous dinners to secure relationships with the most influential men in our county and I soon understood that, since I was the lady of the house, he expected there to be some natural order in our life together, an organised life. He expected natural order in how our possessions were displayed. Silver or porcelain tableware, gold-painted glass, polished wood. All items I'd come into owning and therefore never paid the slightest attention to.

Another thing no one told me is that once you've invited a man to share your bed he disappears. No one explained this part of marriage to me. You get married and become tethered to a plot of land and a man. You become just another piece of furniture and he disappears. He administers lands, counts money, and you manage a house. Tethered to the house and to him, to those stones, to that mortar, to those four beams. This you are, and this you will always be: you turn into dry wood, straw that crackles, wool that itches. Only at night, every once in a while, do you recover your body, whenever his hands appear to knead it and move it and turn it to liquid. Until then, inert. Before and afterwards.

I started to live for those visits, when my husband showed up drunk and excited and threw himself on top of me. If that was the only way I existed, what better way was there? Only then did everything make sense. I waited time and time again for that act of recognition.

For the possibility that his gaze would convert me into something more than livestock, something more than a chair. During the brief spell when all power rested on me, I was a queen with my sparkling crown and each drop of blood that pulsed through my veins was liquid mercury. I could have killed an animal in one bite, not so much because he was mine but rather because I finally existed, and therefore so did words, rhythms and language. In that crack in time, for that instant.

I'd been married for only a short time when my body began to swell, and it happened quickly. My skin became more delicate and softer, and its aroma changed. My hair, previously of an ill-defined colour, turned darker, and everything around me acquired a different consistency, like the skin of a piece of fruit when it ripens, just before exploding. It was in those days when I most desired him and most begged of God for him to stay with me, because nothing else sufficed. He protested, complaining he couldn't always be at home, that he had matters to attend to. I clenched my teeth, it was never enough. I tugged my hair into braids, knotting them above my ears, braids that made my temples taut. That way I could feel *something* anchoring me to this world, instead of the sensation that I was going to float into the sky from so much need.

It was when my godmother came to visit and noticed my mother's impassiveness that she took me off to a corner and revealed what was so obvious to everyone else: 'You're pregnant, child, how could you not have known?'

5. CALLE HERMOSILLA (NOW)

Sometimes I go to Zara stores. I take care not to do it as often now that I'm in Madrid. When I feel the need, I carefully plan when and where, always on a workday between ten and twelve o'clock, at shops in expensive and peaceful neighbourhoods with streets in a grid and white buildings with façades that look like whipped cream where I won't be bothered by other customers or shop clerks. I try to dose out these excursions, but when in need I drag myself from hunting apparel stores to Viennese-style coffeeshops until I arrive at my personal temple. At the precise moment before entering I pause to savour the thrill gushing through me at the threshold of the security detectors.

Yes, Zara stores are an offering for me, they are as priceless as a carefully-polished jewel. Zara stores are my sapphires, I take them out for a stroll only on special days. They are akin to a homage, the equivalent of a relaxing hot bath. When I go there, the first thing that hits me is the air conditioning, which, instead of driving me away, makes me feel protected. Zara stores are my personal amniotic fluid. I bob along their bone-coloured floors, their surface areas of one thousand, two thousand, three thousand square metres, evenly distributed with great care, over several floors. There is nothing safer than this space.

I walk numbly in regular circles around the garments. I never look at the clothes, although I pretend to. I feel the weight of textures from the fall-winter season, taking wide and slow steps. I don't stop. It looks like I'm contemplating the fake cashmeres, the wools, the plastic buttons, the sweaters grouped according to a comprehensive range of colours that looks like the rainbow flag. I simulate being just another customer. I'm incredibly good at pretending. I look like an unoccupied woman with free time just moseying around between brunch and a session of facial radiotherapy. As I wander, the Ibiza-style chill-out playlist doesn't bother me, the easy listening version of Nirvana's 'Come As You Are' has no effect on me, that's not why I'm here.

While I appear to be a leisurely customer in the posh neighbourhood of Salamanca, some Tuesday morning at the end of summer, the scent of the store – a crisp blend that's difficult to describe – makes my heart rate speed up and my breath quicken.

When at last it hits me in waves, I steady myself by grabbing onto a rack of hangers with sherbet-coloured jerseys so I don't fall, weak with emotion. I'm addicted to Zara air freshener. Its scent transports me.

My vision blurs and then it happens. I'm flooded by images of glasses of white wine on the shores of the river Seine, a forest in summer, iridescent bottleflies buzzing around me. I can see a stream the colour of green glass and how it falls in a cascade. I watch my feet pale in colour as they penetrate the cold water. The sound of girls laughing in the distance. A bowl of raspberries at the door of a cabin in the countryside.

A bookshelf filled with leather-bound volumes where I spend rainy mornings in silence. On this particular day, created only for me, it's 1994 and I'm an art history student specialising in the Italian Renaissance. I wear my hair in a ponytail and I feel all snuggly in an untreated-wool jumper. My long, thin fingers turn the pages of an ancient treatise, and I'm about to meet Evan or Nathaniel – the name varies from day to day; that doesn't matter, what matters is that he will be my husband. I see him across the room: a strong masculine presence. In my daydream, he doesn't always have a face. Most often he's simply a sketch with medium-length hair, tortoiseshell glasses and very long arms and legs. His body type is always based on the same man, the Englishman, and sometimes he has the Englishman's smile, but I don't want to think about him right now. I only want to think about Evan or Nathaniel, about how we look at each other from opposite sides of the room and how he walks over. He asks me about a book, he has a deep voice, and I blush and shrink into my jumper. One second later, another image: a sojourn in Edinburgh, a postgraduate degree in speculative thought. Evan or Nathaniel is wearing a tweed jacket with a hoodie underneath. He's let his beard grow out and he kisses me lovingly and holds my face in his hands. His gaze is so pure that when he asks me to come with him to visit his family in Finland, where they live, my chest bursts with love and peace. Then comes the proposal: should we stay there to live in Helsinki? We're both so at ease in the city and we can progress in our careers. We look each other in the eye, we think of a future in common, and timidly confess to each other what we really want: two children, which we have the following year, two beautiful blond boys. We're young, attractive and adventurous parents who walk through wheat fields in summer, the two toddlers scampering around us. We eat cheese and grapes freshly picked from the vine. We make love slowly several times a week, we have friends who design jewellery, who make politically committed electronic art, who are concerned about their mobile devices being monitored, who talk about climate change. I see us all on holiday in a shared house in Sicily, sitting around a set table, smiling and drinking local wine, taking care of our babies together, laughing into the evening.

The fragrance inside Zara is dispersed through manual vaporisers, but it's also connected to the air conditioning that wafts into every corner and impregnates all the clothes. The scent of fresh flowers, wood and some type of incense makes its way to my pituitary gland and fills me with false memories that I so desperately wish were real. Occasionally, when I can't conceal that I'm in a slump and some shop assistant annoyingly approaches me, I feel a ferocious rage begin to rise in my body, a rage that burns like a blue hydrogen flame, a wild rage that blinds my vision and could cause me to hit someone. Only through superhuman strength am I finally able to control myself. Only the exact mixture of Ativan and Prozac. Right at that moment, as I lose everything I never even had, that never even existed – Evan, our children, all our friends – as I lose that house I so elaborately decorated with handwoven rugs and French dishes, as it all fades, I end up bawling my eyes out in some Zara somewhere in the city. I *deserve* that life. Why don't I have it? Who stole it from me?

On those days, the worst days, I have to stop by a Vips for a hot chocolate, or some fried Oreos, or eggs benedict with béarnaise sauce, my face bathed in tears after so many days without eating. Only that calms me down.

On other days, the more bearable ones, when I can make it back from my inner voyage, I take solace by thinking about how there are 2,232 Zara stores around the world and they all smell exactly the same. The one in London, the one in Dubai, the one in São Paulo. I don't have to travel anywhere. There's no need. Here, between the patent leather boots and the cherry-coloured lip gloss, I've got it all.

V. DEBORAH & THE FEVER

The pregnancy was tiresome and difficult. Like a well-oiled machine, the servants threw themselves into taking care of me. The maids bent over backward to provide me with everything I needed. Since the only thing I could stomach was fish from the river – everything else had no flavour for me – each morning someone from the staff went out fishing and came back with trout or barbel, which the cook prepared for my breakfast, lunch and dinner. I never tired of eating fish, despite the disgust it caused in my husband, who put up with my cravings purely because an heir was on the way and this was my time. The sheets were changed every afternoon because I couldn't handle the weight of even the freshest linens. And so the year went for us, until well into winter, when the first contractions began.

It started with excruciating pain, like a bolt of lightning, and I almost fainted by the bathtub. I immediately thought of my husband, who was out hunting with an affluent neighbour. I could feel the cold floor and my forehead moist, sticky to the touch like a slug, and someone went to call the midwife. They laid me down in bed right away. The midwife was accomplished and quick, she lost no time. She told me that I would have no troubles given my constitution, and started to give orders.

They brought perfumes and hot water, rags and healing herbs, and they told me to breathe. Breathe, they said. Hold on, they said, and I felt a flame rising through my skin from the bottom of my feet, burning and freezing me at the same time. I asked for water and ice, water and ice, I'm burning up, and then I was freezing cold and everything hurt. Eternities went by and I heard voices. You are strong, you can do it, you can do it, and all my weight felt concentrated in my belly, and I saw serpents and fire, they intermingled with flashes of green and yellow light the colour of bile. I felt something forming between my legs like mud, and it grew with scales and a forked tongue, and I asked them to take it away, take it away now. Later, the disfigured face of the midwife and only some whispers, 'she has a high fever, she won't hold out much longer', and a sweet and repugnant smell at the end, which at the time I didn't understand, but would later recognise: it was the smell of decay and death. It would be many years before I identified that smell again.

When my husband returned, I'd already been told that I'd given birth to a dead baby boy. My husband never again returned to my bed. He'd bet on the wrong horse, I could see it in his eyes. I knew that I disgusted him and nothing else could be done.

I don't remember much more about the following weeks. Only that when I recovered and the colour came back to my cheeks I called for him and we met in his library, the room where he finalised business deals.

'You have acquired my lands and my money, but it seems we won't be having any heirs, I told him. 'If it suits you for us to live like this, hardly seeing one another, so be it. But let us at least speak candidly and agree upon how to go about it.'

My husband turned his back on me. Men are like that. I remember it as if it were today.

'I'd like to speak with you,' he said. 'You are a God-fearing woman and it's your duty to provide me with children. That seems unlikely, at least for the time being, and I don't think you want a divorce. Am I right? The mere mention has turned you as white as a ghost, it frightens you so. Alas, blessed one! But have no fear for me, my lineage will be passed down. Even if shameful in nature, let it be clear.' Then he whipped around and looked me in the eye. He inhaled deeply before uttering his next words, which would change everything. 'I have an illegitimate son.'

I gritted my teeth to keep from crying or showing my alarm. I counted. One, two, three. I counted the blades of grass I could see from the window. I felt a heaviness in the air, lead weight collapsing on my shoulders, my youth ending in one fell swoop, and I asked:

'What's his name?'

6. PLAÇA DE JAUME SABARTÉS (BEFORE)

The balcony is sunny. It's one of those typical end-of-spring days in Barcelona: humid, fresh and filled with light. That's why I'm out here, enjoying the morning. The flat is small and cheap, considering it's right downtown. True, the walls are really thin with patches of dampness, but there's also this nice balcony, which is its best feature. That's what the real estate agent said when I went to see it, 'It has a balcony!' And that's why he raises the price every year, as if he were personally annoyed that someone should enjoy themselves here, as if imposing his own personal tourist tax on me. That's why, whenever I can, I set up camp here, as if it were an elusive luxury, a Thai spa, and I take in the views. It hasn't been long since they finished renovating the square. Not many people know that hidden beneath the pavement there are some Iberian remains from the Laietani who populated this city: pieces of ceramic, bronze marbles and other metal objects – scalpels and cauteries – to treat the ill. The city council decided not to halt the construction project and instead had everything covered with tarpaper and large slabs of shiny stone, over which

49

now traipse the tourists and the few locals left in the neighbourhood.

From the position I'm in, reclining on my chair, I can see the sea and watch the airplanes fly overhead at regular intervals. As I hold up a book that I'm trying to concentrate on reading, I can't help but notice we need to do something about the patches of dampness, they've caused cracks in the cement render of the low wall. The paint has blistered, and by merely passing my pinkie finger along the wall it crumbles readily. Underneath, sand. These damp spots are starting to add up, I think. I didn't use to care about them when I lived alone, but living with someone else means the balcony simply cannot be in such a state.

Ever since you moved in with me, many things have changed around here. All as if in a state of slumber, like when something happens without one knowing quite how or why. You moved in three months after we met, and now the walls are ivory white, there's a new table and chairs – somewhat wobbly but they look good – and a woven wool throw on the sofa that gives a time-honoured and soothing feel to the flat. Inside it smells like home cooking, and I barely pick up a book any more. I suppose this is domesticity, because although I've had other boyfriends I've never lived with anyone before. There are things that have changed, yes. I read less, not as much as I used to. A relationship brings about these changes: you concentrate less, you work less, you watch more movies on the sofa, you get caught up in preposterous conversations about the day-to-day: which fruit to buy, where you stashed the light bulbs, whose turn it is to wash the dishes.

We have things. We have a whole lot of things. We have a piano, an infinite number of books, postcards sent from Berlin, hiking boots, scarves and flannel shirts, thick wool sweaters, I don't know, so much stuff. We have steamed mussels, stews that take hours to cook, carefully, over a slow flame, as if they involve real craftsmanship. I've even given you a plant. It was after a misunderstanding, although now I've forgotten what the misunderstanding was about. More or less. Something is happening to me that's never happened before, in this relationship that's so stable and full of future prospects: it's hard for me to gauge what is happening to us. You ask me how I feel and I get confused, the answers escape me like the damp sand on the balcony, I'm annoyed by having to explain myself, by the fact that you don't see things from my perspective. I think it's during this time that I start to take tranquilisers. Sometimes the misunderstandings are like whirlpools of murky water that suck me down and from which I cannot escape. And if I don't escape from them, I can't sleep. And you say that we shouldn't go to sleep feeling angry. Sometimes, the separateness of another person's body operates in curious ways, and I wake up at midnight and look at your face without recognising it. One of my coworkers at the office once told me that it happened to her during her first son's childhood: she'd wake up and find him next to her bed, just looking at her, and seeing the face of a boy by her pillow would make her jump with fright. She didn't recognise her own son. I've given birth to a relationship, I think, and I laugh to myself as if the thought were a cruel prank. I feel guilty, suddenly. But really, when we don't understand one another, all I want is for everything to get better again. To once again feel at peace, like I do on this summer day.

Your silhouette is well-proportioned and harmonious, I muse. It's what I like about you. I like your pale eyes, your height. I've paired off with a handsome, respectable man. All the women in my life say so. My mother, who's always so critical, likes you. She told me that you are a trustworthy man, the type that are hard to come by. She liked when I told her you walked me home the first time we went out, you called me the next day and invited me to eat at your place and you even cooked. I've noticed you like to do things with your hands, it relaxes you. Today you say you want to cut my hair, and although I actually don't want you to, it's too complicated to explain how I like the ritual of going somewhere unfamiliar, the smell of perfume, the mindless feminine chatter, and the feeling of walking out renewed, as if I were a different person. I start to tell you this, but you laugh at me a little, I realise I seem frivolous to you sometimes. But you love me, this I know, I can see it in your eyes. This type of love can't be faked. You like being a caretaker and feeling as if our house is a home to be looked after, being responsible and adult, like a man from a bygone era. If I didn't know you, I would think you were a conservative man.

At night, when everything is calm and my body feels tired, I like to hug you from behind without waking you up. It makes me feel complete. This is the time of day when I convince myself you are going to save me from the errors I've made in my life. From the mistakes, the lost time, from the people who haven't treated me right.

And now, in this sunny moment, I hear you say my name and I turn around, and I'm surprised to see it was a trick so you could take a picture of me with your phone. Years later, that photo will be proof that I lived through what's happening right now, it really took place. I see myself in that photo, with my torso twisted toward the camera, sitting on a rickety old chair, on that balcony covered in damp spots, with a book in my hand, wearing a white t-shirt and sunglasses, my bare feet, smiling at you. At you. I see proof of that moment I will no longer be able to recall.

Immediately thereafter, content and at ease, I try to go back to reading my book, try to regain this lost habit, but you come out onto the balcony, you have to run something by me. That's when I notice you're letting your beard grow out. You no longer want to be the boy with sideburns, I suppose. You want to leave behind something juvenile and become a responsible adult, a gentleman. I realise this, although it might be imperceptible to you, and I'm filled with tenderness. You call me darling, you show me that you need me. You always ask me to help you with everything, you consult every detail with me: the trousers you buy, the invoice you submit to the administration. You want me to keep the accounts, you want my advice concerning your career, where to aim, my opinion is the most important. This gives me a sense of power I've never felt before, an unexpected strength. This energy rising from my stomach makes me feel steadier, calmer. When I place orders at IKEA, or I have to call up the electrician because the wiring is shoddy, I refer to you as 'my husband'. Me! My friends would die of laughter if they knew. Me who has always made a getaway from anything remotely domestic, the one who used to get bored when people started talking about curtains and parquet flooring. But even though you aren't my husband, I crave that anchoring, that word solidifies what I need from you, and by saying it, 'my husband', this sensation in my stomach becomes stronger, more present, and I focus on it so it grows. *My husband*, I think, and I get up to set the table for lunch because I've lost track of my reading again, and someone has to make a salad because, otherwise, we'll never eat.

VI. DEBORAH &
THE BLACK MARBLE

All men are alike. This truism took me a while to learn, and I consider it now as I gaze upon my dead husband, years later in London, lying on the black marble table in his library. The clichés women say, murmured in confidence in our parlours, tend to be true. All men are alike, but more than anything they are so predictable. There he is, my husband, dressed like a gentleman, laid out on a black marble table covered by a purple velvet cloth, just as he had requested. His new-money tastes obliged me to bite my tongue while the wake was being organised. The scene is hideous, grotesque, so far-removed from the austerity of our faith: a man weighing more than twenty-three stone, now the colour of wax, laid out on velvet, looking like a turkey about to be boned.

The table showed up during one of my husband's absences, a black monstrosity the size of a bull. The maids promptly explained that it was a marble desk. He had chosen Portoro, an Italian marble, they said, with gold veining. It's a noble material, the most expensive, one of them whispered. She was pretty as a flower, I'd hired her only to tempt him. I became more and more amused to see how, when he deigned to come home, he would disappear into nooks and crannies of the house to fornicate with the maids, like the beast he was.

Now I touch the polished black stone, which reflects no light. I touch the polished stone, cold as the bottom of a lake. I imagine all the sweat that went into fulfilling the whim of this nouveau-riche peasant from the provinces. It's ghastly, I think. I order one of the girls to change the water in the lilies because they're withering and it depresses me. I don't want withered flowers when all the guests arrive. Members of Parliament, entrepreneurs, livestock farmers. I'll have to attend to them all.

It took me some time, but after we stopped sharing a bed, I finally understood that I'd married a man too similar to my father: someone who knew the hard and heavy labour of farming, who'd pulled himself up by his bootstraps. I had a lot of time during his absences to reflect upon what had become of me. All I had, in fact, was time. I could finally think for myself. My choice of a husband makes sense only as such. I confused his capacity for survival and his upward mobility for manliness. How foolish of me! If I had understood it before, I would have been spared from what came thereafter. My husband, like my father, had been forced to carve out a future. He knew about horses, cattle and land, he wasn't merely a city man born into property owning. He was a man from the countryside, he'd known the soil all too well. That mud underneath his fingernails, that stench of manure. Which is why he had wanted to own things. Oh, how he'd wanted them. But not just any type of things, only the best. Silks, spices, gold, exquisite food, bubbly wines. Things to distance him from his origins. Once he had married me, once he became more than a simple farmer on the up – like his father and grandfather had been – he secured a good fortune for himself. And he wasn't going to settle for that alone: he wanted power as well.

It was summertime when, after spending some days in London, he arrived home with the news that I had become the wife of a baronet. I didn't ask, I didn't have to. It was clearly an asinine title that he'd acquired from some bootlicking courtier in exchange for a good part of my dowry. I didn't protest, I understood.

My husband. As the altar candles drip at his wake I contemplate his belly swollen from all the wine and capon. I think of the political dinners, the other women. He thought I didn't notice, or worse — that I didn't care. Men are so predictable and I, finally, had learned the art of dissimulation.

'We're going to the city,' he said.

'To Bath?'

'No, wife. To London. I've been chosen by Malmesbury to become a Member of Parliament. I found the perfect house for us, right near Westminster, and I need you there.'

My head spun with joy. London? Finally? Even so, I was afflicted by doubts. I'd only just made my peace with the house, the maids, the changes in season.

'I won't go.'

'Of course you will. I wouldn't allow you to stay here and turn into a yokel. Where would that leave me? You have a new occupation: entertaining the wives of the other Members of Parliament. We must gain their confidence and I need you for that. You've learned to run the house well, you're clever and quick. We must join forces to organise our new life.'

Henry Moody, you lie dead before my eyes and I've almost forgotten everything. I've forgotten our first mornings together, your blond beard, those stubby, strong hands you always detested and I loved so much in the beginning. I've forgotten the scent of sage on your body, before you turned into this ridiculous turkey in front of me now, before you decided to become that parvenu everyone listened to simply because you were *from* the countryside, and precisely for that reason they figured you must be honest. People are stupid, sometimes I forget. Men don't change and people are stupid.

'I have only one condition. The boy comes with us.'

A thick and dirty silence followed, like a puddle. I could see him quickly doing calculations in his head, and how he automatically sought the exits from the room: where the doors were, how long it would take him to reach the nearest one. He'll be a good Member of Parliament, I thought.

'Deborah, the boy has a mother.'

'No. I've tolerated your infidelities. You've sold my lands at a loss. You've publicly humiliated me. If we are to start anew, I want a son.'

'And just what do you want me to do? Abduct him? Have you gone mad?'

'You are a baronet and a politician now, isn't that right? Lock her up. She's a married woman and an adulteress. It won't be too hard, now that you have power. We will keep the boy and he will come to London with us. He will take your name, Henry Moody. He's hardly two years old, I'll be his mother from now on. That is my only condition.'

Days later, a nondescript woman with gloomy features showed up at my house with the most beautiful little boy known to humankind, with blond curls and almond-shaped eyes, who looked up at me, very seriously, barely two handbreadths from the ground.

Lord, now that you have abandoned me, I hope you forgive my sins. I know they abound. I know you have had to make an effort, but such is love, one effort after another, and I have devoted myself to you. If there is anything left to atone, forgive me one sin, tell me where I am and remove me from here, from under the earth.

You know well this story that led my husband and I to live in London. We didn't take anyone from the countryside with us except Henry, not one servant. My husband's only demand was the marble table, him and his things! All those many things we accumulated thereafter as a symbol of his new status, nothing but possessions, and the first was that table pulled along by three horses, three poor animals that had to be put down no sooner had they arrived at the gates of the city, exhausted by their journey, which had taken longer than usual. I overheard the coachman discussing how the bottom broke out from under the carriage every three or four days due to the enormous weight being transported.

7. CARRER NOU DE SANT CUGAT (BEFORE)

There are things that make me hesitate sometimes. One morning a couple of weeks ago, on our way to the neighbourhood market, we crossed paths with some people we see from time to time, dehydrated and pale, sunglasses on and laughing loudly. It was clear they were on their way back from an afterparty, probably the one on Nou de Sant Cugat, and I noticed the look on your face, the disdain, as if they smelled bad. 'What a gang of freaks,' you said, and I nodded, without much conviction. I didn't quite understand the comment, but decided not to remind you that you and I had met at a bar where we both used to get pretty drunk and where cocaine went around. But that day, on a narrow street twisting toward the market, the tallest guy in the group waved at me from afar, a subtle gesture. He smiled at me sweetly, and I remembered a night several years ago at a rooftop terrace on Ausiàs March street. Someone I knew lived in a shared flat there, five or six flatmates in one of those two-hundred-square-metre apartments in Eixample Dret you could rent back then; not any more, of course. I remembered him standing very close to me, I remembered his breath on me and our conversation about Aztec pyramids or some other nonsense, one of those conversations you have at five o'clock in the morning when nobody cares any more and someone's standing too close for it to matter. I didn't wave back, I turned away so that you – my *husband* – wouldn't see him, and I didn't say anything about them, about how I know them, the tall guy in particular. How could I tell you about that? Instead, I felt like my new life had no room for any of that, my new life demanded purity, dedication, sacrifice. I don't know why, but my new life requires a special type of discipline. But today is another day, a cold and quiet midday in winter, and the sun is shining weakly through the window. I like winter, I think as I take out our good tablecloth and start to set the table. You are in the kitchen, today you are going to be in charge of dinner and I feel an electric charge in the air. I know you're nervous because you've invited several friends over to discuss a new project. After the surge in demonstrations in many cities, you, who were already a good public speaker and have people skills, began to realise that something is going to happen, something that could spark something else much more important. You've explained it to me several times and your eyes light up with excitement: the Asturian miners' strike last summer was a turning point, a point of no return. Everything always starts in Asturias, and now it's time to get organised. If we do it right, it will be time for a new nation. I tell you you're right, I know you need me to say it, this could be a good incentive for change. I know that you're tired of selling projects to an increasingly erratic and debilitated administration. We're at the height of the economic crisis and people like you, with somewhat ambiguous university degrees and not much practical experience, abound. It doesn't matter that you have charisma, that when you talk to someone you make them feel like the most important person in the room, like you did with me that day at the bar; that doesn't do the trick these days. You're tired of not being appreciated, of having to do things you don't like. You tell me this, frustrated, and I hug you and tell you that everything will work out even though I know you've been like this for months, not getting much sleep, worried about your financial future, which is now also mine. We don't discuss that I make more than you, but we both know it. So whatever happens now will be good for your spirits.

I walk over to the kitchen sink and see the shopping bags with the ingredients you'll use to prepare our meal: lamb with sweet potatoes and grilled peppers. Simple and traditional. Nothing unexpected, I think. I know exactly what will come next: we'll cook, listen to vinyls while we prepare a vermouth with potato chips and mussels in escabeche as we await our guests. This is something I like about you, you have lots of friends, people who care about you. You're a man who stands by his friends, and they come over often. I enjoy living like this, it relieves me from my Monday to Friday routine in Plaça de les Glòries, and from the greyness of a life that could be uninspiring. I no longer go to bars unless I'm with you, true, and when I see my girlfriends these days it's here at home more than anywhere else, always with their significant others. These friends and I, who weren't exactly domestic, now only get together in our living rooms, and very rarely at that. And my other friends are a distant memory. They used to call me up to get together, but building a partnership takes effort and dedication, so first they slid into the background and now they've settled into a very discreet third place. But your friends are nice, I like them, they make me laugh. Not feeling the need to make an effort relaxes me, having it all served up on a plate. Yes, I've got used to this life. After we eat I know what will follow: five men will sit around our table and discuss a political project for hours, until late into the night. Democratise democracy. Storm the institutions. Gain control of the narrative. Everything is a mission, has a sequence. Meanwhile, I will focus on something else: clearing the table. Even so, none of this plagues me. No, not yet.

It's true that sometimes, at night, I secretly yearn for the life I had before I met you, when I went dancing, when I was someone else, someone similar but different. I don't tell anyone, don't even admit it to myself. A life of my own, I don't say it. My own, I don't even think it. It's true that there are things I don't tell anyone, least of all my girlfriends, who I now see at these homecooked dinners. I don't tell them that after the first few months we rarely have sex. That our misunderstandings have turned into arguments, and when we argue I always have to be the one to give in and ask for forgiveness, because I was wrong. Say you're sorry, do us both a favour, how hard is it? I think, and then my sobs and a feeling of anguish like my throat being slit. You agree to accept my apology, reluctantly, and then we make up by giving each other gifts. After that first plant, which grows on the balcony, magnificently, I'm almost always the one to give the gifts, and I know why. Because it's always my fault that we argue. That's the undeniable truth. Ever since we've been together my temperament has started to sour, despite the love. In the heat of our arguments, during which I can't organise my thoughts or ideas, I'm short-tempered. I defend myself from any possible attack by using words and gestures I don't recognise in myself. I'm a rabid cat ready to lash out at anything. When you have turbulent days that make you feel vulnerable, you ask for my advice and you keep me close. I become susceptible, jealous of everything I can't control, jealous of the space, the air, of everything worthy of your attention that's not me. Sometimes, I would consume you if I could. I would inhale you like the fog that envelops the city now and again, from end to end. I never quite remember how it all starts, but after all the tears and the anxiety that slices through the centre of my solar plexus, the horror finally ends and I can feel my skin like new, regenerated, shiny as a scar. Some days I secretly take a Valium in the bathroom and then I cry less. After our last fight, and because you want to set things right between us, you suggest that I go out and see my friends, the ones I almost never see any more, and I know that it's an offering, an olive branch, I know you want to take care of me and love me, and I feel awash with joy, disproportionately so, as if I'd been given a soft and silky puppy dog, and I pray that everything turns out well, I consciously prepare myself for that moment, because of how rare it is. There's something unsaid that has settled in, and I know exactly what it's all about. My friends are raucous, when they drink they don't let anyone else get a word in edgewise, and they trivialise everything. They spend too much money on junk, and compared to you they don't even seem like adults, but more like whiny little kids, even though we're all the same age. And the few times we *do* get together with them you look at me out of the corner of your eye and grab my hand and smile at me, and even so, despite the fact that you stoically endure it, I tend to feel embarrassed so I cut back on these encounters, I space them out more and more so I don't feel clumsy and out of place. Only when I am with you am I where I should be.

That night, the night you suggest I see my friends, will be different, I can tell. Everything is calm and I feel relaxed and good. I'm prepared to enjoy myself in the company of my friends and my boyfriend, and there's nothing wrong with this picture. Everything is in order, you've reserved a table at a place that's reliable and popular, like you, and your telephone rings and you pick up while

I'm putting on makeup in the bathroom, and although at first I think the call is from someone at the restaurant, to confirm the table, I immediately realise that it's something about the Citizens' Party platform in the making, and I deduce that the conversation will go on for at least twenty minutes, so I make use of the time to primp more meticulously. I blow-dry my hair, pin it up with bobby pins and choose a short white dress that my girlfriends say makes my legs look long, and some low-heeled sandals you picked out for me on our trip to Vienna, some old sandals from the 1930s with leather edging in the shape of a wave, and I wait for you by the door, all dolled up and perfumed, wait for you to finish your conversation, and when you hang up and finally look me up and down you say, choking back your laughter: Honey, is that what you're going to wear? Can't you see that you look like a hooker? And you say this shamefully, not because of the words you used, but because you're talking to me as if you were talking to a little girl, to a moron, a girl who lacks the ability to distinguish between good and bad, and it's true that I didn't notice, I must be an idiot or something because I didn't notice. And, feeling stunned, I walk back to the bedroom, take off the short white dress and put on something else, a boxy linen shirt and pleated trousers, and you appreciate this gesture and kiss me and hold out your hand, and although everything goes back to normal I'm suddenly very tired, and I start to count all the things we have, we have orange juice in the morning, we have lots of books, so many books, we have clothes, gas for the winter (which is surely going to be cold), we have a Peruvian wool blanket, conference invitations, tickets to the movies and the theatre, we have bottled water, glass cleaner, wet towels, dust bunnies under the sofa, we have ceramic tiles, a marble table, we have

VII. DEBORAH & THE WATER

If I could say something to that girl so eager to die, so many years in the future, so far from here, in another port city, I would tell her to have no fear. Dying is not so bad.

Take a look at me, Lord, here, underground. You've refused to give me an answer, forcing me to arrive at the conclusion that I am dead. I'm obviously dead, although I can feel the salty sand around me. What a strange body you've provided me with. And, incidentally, how many times have I died before? Two, three? Fifty? I remember no other life beyond the one I relate now. Dying doesn't save you from anything, death doesn't redeem you from your sins. I'm sorry, Lord, if saying so is a sacrilege. It's hard to grasp, but once you know it, this is what Christian liberation is all about. Dying didn't save me. It doesn't matter what the great disseminators of your word say. Forgive me, Father, as you have forgiven me so many times. My Father, my beloved Lord.

You know the story about all my deaths so, dear Lord, admit it's true: I did not have an easy life. I didn't expect another obstacle in my path, that test you put me to after my husband's death. I didn't expect poverty. He squandered everything I had and, little by little, the creditors came to pay their visits, which didn't entirely take me by surprise. A woman who runs her own house is capable of predicting these things. I wasn't, by that point, a complete idiot. Nor was I an innocent woman any longer. At most, I could be accused of a certain devotion to your word and a righteous life, nothing more. Everything that distanced me from my previous life bestowed me with the tranquillity of knowing all I had to do was await divine salvation. I clung to that possibility day and night. Even so, I was forced to descend to the material world all at once. Because there's a big difference between having to water down one's milk in the morning to make gruel, and having absolutely nothing at all. That monumental difference finally arrived. I, who'd come from a family that had it all, was suddenly left with nothing. So we had to leave.

My darling son, my Henry, looked at me with those enormous eyes the colour of an endless salty sea. Here, underground, I still see him as a child, although that time has passed. He must have been seventeen by the time we left London. He moved deftly around the deck of the foul ship that took us away from the city. It is difficult to understand what it means to alter the life of a child, but you, dear Lord, you know the traps of faith. Facing the creditors was one thing, but having to face the Church was something entirely different. How was I to know back then that my refuge – my only space in life, your word, your word of warm psalms, of cherry-coloured stained glass – would be such a great test? That it would demand so much sacrifice?

All that time to myself, first because of my husband's absences and then as a widow, had given me a nest in which to cradle our beliefs. A community, a life. I'd been embraced by other women and able to discuss what was consuming me inside. Why, Father? Why did you charge us with such whole-hearted surrender from the time we were nothing but little lambs? Had I not been able to choose my own son? As a grown woman, without it being imposed upon me by fornication as my husband intended. I remembered the bile-coloured serpents and the fire, that desire I had yearned for so greatly, as if it were pure water. But a thirst like that never leads to anything gratifying. At last I understood. I had been able to choose my own son, and my son had chosen me. Faith must work like this, I whispered to the women I met while my husband was still alive. We whispered these words at dinner parties when they went off to the library to discuss their business deals. Did they think we didn't talk amongst ourselves? Naturally, there was always one sourpuss who didn't join in and whose only reason for being there was to praise the political notions of her husband, but that was the exception. What did you *think* would happen, dear God, when you granted us the power of speech and of reason? That you could deny us from making choices? Once we understood what real desire is and how it takes shape, how could we not realise what truly mattered was our right to decide?

Poverty had given us readiness and your word gave us a purpose. We'd found our peers through our faith. We'd realised it too late, we were already mature women, but our social condition was fixed: we were poor in terms of possessions, but we continued to be aristocrats in our heads. We never thought they would come for us. What more could they take from us now? We'd already been stripped of everything.

Foolish women. I think of my Henry and of our crossing in that ship filled with rats, the creaking wood, and all of us huddled together. I was struck by the need to avenge my husband for his wheeling and dealing: I had to abandon London in twenty-four hours, to set an example. An example of what? It didn't matter. Women always end up being an example, Lord, the Scriptures are a clear exponent of what I mean. Sarah, Hagar and Abigail are not real women. They serve only for a cause, as I must now serve for another.

Decide we would, they couldn't deprive us of that. I wouldn't allow Henry to return to our old lands as a wretch. Besides, they would end up finding us there, too. Some opted for settling in a town somewhere close to a forest and doing your work, dear Lord. But I couldn't do that to Henry. The burden would be too great for him. We had got used to the cobblestone streets. City streets are like your word, they have structure and make sense. I wanted my son to prosper in a better place, our land would be new and spacious, with no secrets. Yes, we would finally establish that new order, by the grace of God, for your kingdom, for our survival and preservation. We were finally nearing you, to seek out our new Promised Land.

8. CARRER DELS VALERO (BEFORE)

Sometimes, like the solid couple we are, especially when we haven't had an argument, we make plans. One of our favourite things to do is to walk around neighbourhoods to which we have no affiliation. So one day you suggest to me in an amusing tone, after finishing up one of your meetings with friends from the burgeoning citizens' formation, which have become more and more frequent on weekends, that we meet up in a posh neighbourhood – why not – the poshest one that we can think of, and take a stroll there, as if we were going for a walk on Mars. 'Let's meet at the Turó park', you say. I don't refuse. I don't tell you how I really feel about that plan. I don't contradict you.

But in my head, as if it were an invocation, I say to myself:

…Nothing frightens me more than neighbourhoods in the Zona Alta of Barcelona on a Sunday afternoon: the area between the church of San Gregorio Taumaturgo, Modolell and Juan Sebastián Bach streets, the red-brick buildings from the 1940s and 1950s, their striped mint-green and cream-coloured awnings, those huge apartment buildings with their large glazed vestibules, windows that reflect the winter sun in the Turó park at sunset, water lilies decaying in the ponds that the babies of Sant Gervasi and Tres Torres approach at a crawl beneath the not–so–attentive gaze of their Latina nannies, chatting furiously on their phones with teenage children they've left behind in their own countries, as they yank on the leash of a Cocker Spaniel that they likewise ignore. So what?

Nothing frightens me more than those three- and four-storey houses, where the homes of families with double-barrelled surnames alternate with fertility clinics, pastry shops and rotisseries frequented by engineers, real estate developers and conservative journalists who do each other favours in exchange for a couple of cases of Veuve Clicquot and two hundred grams of smoked Norwegian salmon. Nothing frightens me more because there's no one out on those curving streets, not even in broad daylight. There's never a soul to be seen in the Zona Alta, only brick buildings and some recently-installed security cameras, so that if you get raped by some snob who can get away with it – because if you get raped up there, girlfriend, chances are he can get away with it – no one will come to your rescue, not even the doormen who work on weekends, the ones who don't even get Christmas Day off. Nobody will hear you, no one will come out from the deserted florist's, or from the Italian clothing shops open on public holidays, the ones that defy the regulations of the Generalitat in the hope that some bored lady will turn up and try something on. Your bloodcurdling screams will be ignored while Bosco, Álvaro or Yago sticks an iron pole up your cunt, you fucking whore. Nothing but your howls will be heard, nothing but the warble of some starling or, at most, the soft purring of a bottle-green Jaguar as it rolls out from some building, right between Modolell and Juan

Sebastián Bach streets, right where that lovely oyster bar is that's so sublime you've always wanted to take your parents there for a special occasion, maybe a birthday.

VIII. DEBORAH &
THE GLASS HOUSE

There is nothing quite like being a widow. Dear Lord, grant me this extravagance, just once more. I could never say it in Saugus, in the Massachusetts Bay, the first port where we settled when we got off the boat. I could say so little there at first, but now that I'm dead what difference does it make? Saugus gave us the promise of another life, a different life, at last. Aside from our aspirations and exhaustion, what I really recall is that it wasn't so different from any other beginning. That is to say, there are those who cross the ocean simply in search of a roof and a warm bed, while there are those who do so to devote themselves to God. In my case, the fact that I was able to refocus on the small things was what gave me solace and order. There was a new land and it was our job to organise it.

Strong arms were needed, and my poor Henry broke his back from the start working for a blacksmith in our village, which had kept its Indian name. My little boy of blond curls, now a man, after having witnessed so much decay and death on our trip, had been forever changed and was content doing manual labour from dawn to dusk. He, whose destiny had been to follow our noble lineage, this boy of smooth skin, had developed callouses from working with metal, as if serving a prison sentence, pure labour with the blow of a hammer.

But me? I was the queen of my house, a little grey house of wood in the centre of town. I planted vegetables in my garden, which didn't grow easily because the soil was different, the climate was different, and I kept a home with just two rooms. I had life to spare, I did, even though I was already considered to be an old lady. My poor young neighbours were condemned to give birth to child after child, many of whom died, haunting me with that same sweet smell. I crossed paths with them on my way to the market, where I exchanged lettuce and carrots for bread and cheese. They walked along silently, without looking up, their bonnets low on their brow, like a bluebell flower when it dries up.

My intention was for us, the women who were fervent followers of your word, to be able to live freely without having to hide our faith, to live a righteous and useful life. Utility is a virtue that had been instilled in us from the start. I felt good about it. We needed those limits in the New World, in that land with so much open space. The scents, the plants, the animals. The New World. I'd read about it in books, but nothing compares to having it unfurl before your eyes. The streets there didn't twist and turn; they were straight lines, sharpened like scissors to separate good from evil. At first, so much order comforted me. Nothing compares to structure. Nothing makes sense like the shortest path, straight as an arrow.

But having purpose is one thing; it's something entirely different to have a series of instructions imposed upon you from which you cannot stray. Having order made sense, but, alas, our founders had something more: they had directives. These directives supposedly came from your word and were to be followed to the letter, because, after all, we lived in a new exemplary village. Soon I realised that our walls were built with wood, but they were made of glass, where God saw everything – but that God was not you, dear Father. It was someone more imposing who didn't even give us space to think. The reverend came to see us practically every day, to ask us about our duties. 'People tell me they've seen Henry working too hard. What sins is he atoning for? Dear Deborah, your calling, the calling of the Lord, do you feel it in earnest? How do you know it is real?' I started to feel a tightness in my chest that kept me awake at night. When I closed my eyes I felt as if my eyelids were transparent, and I could see the immense darkness and all of its silence beyond my own flesh. The lack of sleep took its toll on me and it wasn't long before the humidity sank into my bones and they began to ache.

At night, images of the reverend came to me. His hair so dry and blond, like straw, almost transparent. His eyes, a penetrating blue, pierced through mine, all the way to the sockets, and I felt faint from the jitters they gave me. I sensed that this was his ploy, making us believe that he could see through us, that our bodies were made of glass, too. That was how our new Promised Land was to be, our new rules. And I, naturally, was a woman with no husband. There were no walls that could withstand those eyes of ice, not even the walls of an old woman who was alone. Not even my son Henry could protect me from those eyes. Had I crossed oceans to press ahead and reach the Promised Land, just to come up short now? It seemed somewhat excessive from you, my Lord, putting me to the test from the very start.

One day, while I was on my way back from the market, content at having sold some eggs at a good price, I ran into him sprinkling salt at my door.

'I am a pious woman, Reverend, what are you doing sprinkling salt at my doorstep? Have you, by chance, seen the devil on the prowl?'

The reverend smiled with beatitude.

'Why, of course not, Deborah. It's only to protect you from so much activity.' His smile darkened. 'You work too hard. As you well know, one does not work because one believes idleness is a sin, nor to seek some other fruit from her labour, but rather to bring in money, which we know is wrong. It seems to me that you are accumulating too much wealth. Perhaps it would be wise for you to consider how to reinvest in your community.'

I felt something forcing me to speak, like a burning tongue that would scorch me if I didn't let it loose, like a cascade of tears. It was your voice, I suppose, dear Father, dear Lord. I would say you were speaking through me, if this weren't a real confession. I'm a well-educated woman and you know it. It was my voice. My widow's voice, speaking loud and clear.

'Yes, Reverend, but diligent work is a worthy vocation through which a person can provide what she needs for herself and for those who depend on her. Remember that the fruit and possession of goods and wealth are a blessing from God, and must be well utilised. The accumulation of wealth is not prohibited, because the Scriptures allow for it under certain circumstances. Let us not forget Corinthians 12:14.'

We didn't last long in Saugus. A few months later we moved to a much larger farm where I could hire labourers and continue my own work. I so dearly missed my companions with whom I'd read the sacred Scriptures in London, with whom I'd met to discuss our designs and dreams. We moved to an outlying area of the bay, somewhere close to the sea but still green, a different setting where we could live in a house that wasn't made of glass, where I wasn't so exposed, where we could be useful to our society. We went to a fresh, peaceful place with enormous possibilities. A truly pure place where we could start anew. We went to the outskirts of Salem.

9. PLAÇA DE JAUME SABARTÉS (BEFORE)

I am thirty-three years old and you are thirty-seven. We've been together for sixteen months. Two months ago you asked me to stop taking the pill, the one that you yourself had asked me to start taking when we first started going out, because you don't like using condoms.

Like everything in my life as of late, this did not happen exactly as I'd expected. There has been no heart to heart talk or obvious progression in our feelings leading us to realise we want to have a baby together. Instead it feels like a performance directed by someone else. I imagine this from behind my numbness and admire it. I don't understand how we got here. It's like standing under the stream of a warm and pleasant shower and then suddenly, just one degree hotter, the water starts to scald you. What is that slight and imperceptible change? What makes it so intolerable? Perhaps my nerves are on edge, I don't know, but something shifts forever.

A love advice columnist would say that everything happened naturally. The scene is an ordinary scenario any old weekend in the suburbs of Barcelona. A long and narrow yard covered in pale green grass, a two-storey exposed concrete house behind us. I think we're in Esplugues, which is located one hundred metres above sea level and has some ancient estates. I think so, I'm not sure. It could also be Floresta or Mirasol. What do I know? The words get jumbled up and place names sometimes make no sense. The neighbours have just joined us, and therefore this simple meal has turned into a full-fledged plan with four children and six adults. The sheer noise made by the children beats us to a frazzle. All this happens on a fresh June day. The kids run circles around our ankles, someone's carrying firewood and I find myself obliged to talk to the two women next to me, who are tired of chasing after their children. I scan the whole yard to try and understand what my role is in this space. At the other end I see one of the men trying to light a gas burner atop a butane canister.

It's not the first time this has happened, of course. And since it's not the first time, I have started to realise that something occurs to me in situations like these, ordinary everyday situations, with other people. The spectacle of the men in a circle contemplating a gas burner, on their knees, as if it were a holy grail, while they discuss whether to add more fumet or more rosemary, or whether the rice is better when it's been slightly toasted, has started to cause in me a peculiar luminous phenomenon. Specks of iridescent dust appear around my eyes like a beautiful halo that I want to follow, a halo that gives way to a voice, to a new feeling, something pushing me forward and causing in me a tremendous urge to kick each of them in the nape of the neck, covering everything in blood. Sometimes I kick them head on, taking out someone's teeth. One of them gets a fat lip. I watch how it turns blue. Everything unfolds in front of my eyes so realistically until I notice, somewhat disappointed, that the paella continues its course and I sigh. And when the rice starts to bubble and the men get up, feeling proud, I feign a smile of relief to whoever is standing next to me at the time.

Today won't be the day I bash in any of these men's faces. It won't be today. Today, like always as of late, I am well-behaved. Today, the idea hovers over me languidly for a minute and a half until the impulse gives way and I devote myself to drinking more wine than I should. Meanwhile, one of the other two women tells me that she hasn't weaned her older son, even though he eats macaroni with tomato sauce and is old enough to know his ABCs by heart. I nod calmly, feeling how tight my trousers are, my armpits perspiring, and a drop of sweat runs from my bra down to my bellybutton. Plop. A little while later I see how you, my partner, have managed with great skill to light the fire and, along with the rest of the men, are cutting up vegetables to sauté. I ask myself whether I should applaud. I wonder whether that would be the right thing to do. Lately it's not clear to me what the right reaction is because sometimes I'm wrong and I disappoint you, and when that happens the look in your eyes is so different from the fascination that was there when we first met. It makes me disappear and the hole inside me grows and grows, consuming everything, and I become hollow. That's why I now resign myself to simply watching you, it's the safest thing to do, isn't it? And you smile at me knowingly from afar, beaming after having accomplished the task at hand. You made the fire and I smiled. I suppose you've read my smile as something akin to pride. Luckily, I have yet to mess up and my distress finally subsides. You don't know that I detest these meals, you've got used to me pretending that I like them and you relax. You can't tell that I'm faking, smart as you are. Yes, you are smart and perceptive, but only when it serves your purpose. By this point, you've stopped noticing and my deceit is enough for you, and being relaxed and at ease makes you fun and kind. You hug me from behind, you tell jokes, and you make me feel safe and special. Unique, I guess. I look off in the distance, at the sea on the horizon, and a memory emerges like a gulp of salty water.

It's eight years earlier, I am twenty-five years old and it's the middle of summer. In September, I will start to work for the city council after applying for a position in the public sector that was announced in all the newspapers. 'Seeking content writers', the ad said, along with an e-mail address. After three technical exams and an interview, they've called me back to let me know I've been selected, and my friends and I have been celebrating my new job now for several days whenever we get the chance, which isn't that hard given that it's August. My friends, who share a flat on Meridiana avenue, give me everything I could ever want this August in the city. Last night a heavy rain fell, flooding the city. The water reached as far as the Maresme, so we decide not to go to the beach because it will be filled with rats. The last time we went to the beach after a storm they came down from the riverbed and we confused them with small dogs. Yuck, we're not going to make that mistake again.

Although it cools down at night, the sun is strong, so we take turns standing in front of the fan. Someone says we should buy a fan that has a compartment for ice cubes and, voilà, instant A/C. Nobody has money to buy a new fan. We compare our tans to see whose skin is the darkest and we debate between two possible plans for the night: a concert by a band called Los Chicos or the patronage festival of Badalona. Nobody knows, nobody decides. We wear skimpy cotton and Lycra dresses and walk barefoot around the house. We pandiculate like cats as if we were one and the same, trying to shake off a mild hangover.

84

Someone goes into the kitchen and as if by magic brings back some lemonade. I hear the sound of the ice cubes clinking in tall glasses as I stretch out in an armchair in the dining room. Meridiana avenue is less noisy from the ninth floor.

August blankets the city like a premonition: the pollen from the plane trees on the asphalt, the birds first thing in the morning and this sticky humidity. And La Sagrera is, on days like this, the best place to be if you're broke. It's a neighbourhood without tourists in an era in which they've started to arrive in Barcelona on cruise ships, we've seen them on days we go downtown. In just two years this place has filled up with foreign tourists. Don't you know it, someone says, it might as well be Lloret. And they're right. Going to the city centre is like visiting the beach town of Lloret de Mar in my childhood, the same smell of fried onions and reheated waffles, the same sea of sunburned skin, the same sensation of dizziness from all the people and the sun combined, people and sun, people packed together like a tin of sardines, sun in a tin, the shiny tin burning your skin when you try to sit down on a car bonnet at the beach and your mother used to say: keep away from there, can't you see you'll get burned? Keep away from there, your instincts tell you now, not your mother, each time you walk down the Ronda de Sant Pere. I don't tell my girlfriends that, from what I've heard, a large train station is going to be built exactly fifty metres from where we are lying. Someone heard from someone who knows that it's going to be an AVE high-speed rail station, that they've already purchased the tunnel drillers, which will increase the price of flats by at least thirty percent. Now is a good time to buy property, so they say.

Someone rings the doorbell. It's the only one of us who was missing: she just got off the nightshift at a women's shelter and she's really tired. 'She wants to get back together with her ex,' she says, shaking her head. We know that she's talking about a girl from the shelter whose boyfriend broke her jaw. She told us the story the other day, and we say I'm sorry, I'm sorry, and make up a bed for her in another room so she can sleep for a while, and we try to lower our voices, and talk in whispers, but we're too happy. There's too much to do, too much still to invent, we chatter too loudly, and our stupid jokes make us roar with laughter. Eventually she gives up and comes back out to the living room. We decide to go out for an aperitif on Escòcia street, and we fill up a bag with cans of beer. It's still daytime and we've no idea when we'll be back.

We sit idly on a shady terrace. We order lots of food. Someone says she once *literally* had a shag between a rock and a hard place and the cackling kicks off again. I look at my legs, so pale, beneath a loose skirt, and eat some sizzling-hot fried baby squid. I take a sip of beer. I look at the grey pavement, the grey buildings and the deserted city and I am entirely unconscious of the happiness I'm in the midst of. It's like floating in a raft down a mellow river, a smooth mirror along which I glide and never fall, I just sway and rock and bob in place.

That night, at a dance club, I meet a young man – handsome, blond and foreign – who my friends and I baptise 'the Englishman'. I'm wearing a tight floral-print dress and laughing with my girlfriends. He sees me from the other side of the dance floor and approaches to ask me something. We spend three weeks together without leaving my house until he goes back to his country, because he's married, he has two children, and I live in a shared flat near Hospital Clínic. I don't suffer, not even once that whole time. I never manage to forget him.

'Are you all right?' you ask, still clutching me from behind. 'What's wrong? You're so quiet.'

'Nothing.'

We all drink wine and you and the other men keep going back to talking about politics. Since you're in a good mood, you ask my opinion, something you do more and more rarely. I'm tempted to tell you that I don't know, that lately I only think about mountains of blood, geysers of crimson liquid that shower my body, landing in drops, enormous black lagoons of blood in which I submerge myself while everything else occurs. But I don't say that, because today is a good day. I try to focus on the conversation and identify the topic: constitution making processes. Good, I can do that. I can regain the thread. But suddenly one of the women interrupts her partner with a cutting remark about how tired she is of being the only one to take care of their children. This isn't her first nasty comment. I notice a shift in the power dynamics between the couples around us. I promise myself I will never be like that. I tell myself I will never play the role of the angry woman who blames her husband for not taking care of their kids. I will never humiliate you. You grab my hand under the table and squeeze it. You shift your attention back to me and you can sense what I'm thinking. You realise that I am good, I am on your side, and your face is suddenly rapturous with love and you pour everyone another glass of wine. Some spills on the tablecloth, darkens it immediately, forming blue, almost black stains. You laugh, slapping the table, and say to your friend's partner: 'Quit it, can't you see that you're going to scare her? I'm still trying to convince her that forming a family is a good idea.' And everyone laughs and whistles, jovially. It takes me a while to realise that a tectonic plate has just shifted, that somewhere an exoplanet has just turned to dust while all this is happening here, while everyone laughs and I look at you and all the cowlicks in your hair and your clothes smelling of smoke and butane, and you're drunk. Now comes the fun part, someone else says, and everyone laughs again and I think: it's *me*, the chosen one, the mother. And I don't think how perhaps it's too soon, nor do I consider our increasingly frequent and complex fights that contort everything leaving no exit. Our fights are dense and vitriolic, like a sticky labyrinth of tar. But I don't think about that. No, I don't even think about us. I think again about how I'm the chosen one, which is a sign that everything is as it should be, there's no room for doubt. A child will ensure that you stay with me forever. Yes, if I have a child you will never leave me. I am the chosen one, and when you've been chosen it's good news, worth telling, and I have to tell *someone* because *someone* will surely be very happy that this has just happened.

Days later, my head is buried in the pillow and we are fucking mechanically, me with my head on the pillow, and you from behind. I hear the sound of your hips smacking against my backside at a steady rhythm, but our limbs are too heavy, you don't come and neither of us speak. We're sweating from the effort and someone says, 'let's just try again later' and someone else says 'don't talk to me like that, don't be condescending, this isn't my fucking fault'. And I am so far from there, so far away, at least a thousand metres away, at least as far as the bells in the Mercè church tower that chime on Sunday mornings, and where the virgin stands with one foot in the air, stepping forward into the abyss. My weary bronze virgin, the one they remade even bigger to atone for all the sins. My virgin, my angel transformed into a woman, and I'm up there with her and I can see the whole city, and thank goodness, because I know if I'm up there and not in this bed none of this matters, none of this failure.

IX. DEBORAH & SALEM

W as I happy in Salem? It's difficult to say. I no longer know what happiness is, the same way I no longer know what love is. Little is certain to me. I remember my house was more spacious and tidier, light poured into it from an early hour and it had a view of the whole bay. I chose it not because I was sentimental, no, I was a calculating woman: my husband had chiselled away at me, betrayal after betrayal, hardening me. The house was near some plots that had yet to be claimed and my plan was to start accumulating my own land, little by little.

Still, my serenity was debatable. The first obstacle was Reverend Hugh Peter, a man with a gaunt face, pronounced chin and thick hair who you, Lord, managed to place just minutes from my house. Another one of your tests. Another reverend looking for explanations. Nevertheless, Salem was bigger. It was a town of merchants and had an extensive and bustling port, and I could move between my home, the church and the market with relative ease, as long as I respected certain codes.

It wasn't too late, at my age, to learn these codes. A woman exists to be observed, they say. God, you created us mere mortals, with reasoning and the ability to tempt men, but in old age we find consolation, wherein one can escape if she can camouflage herself enough. I was a pious woman who could move between town – where poor farmers worked the hard soil – and the prosperous port, to trade with skill. Oh, Lord, if only you had made me a man. What a great entrepreneur you missed out on! If only I had been Henry, Samuel or David, instead of Deborah, this story would have been quite different. But such was your plan for me, which I followed like a line on a map. Among the codes I learned was to conceal the speed with which I could do mental calculations, or my knack for distinguishing between sizes of sacks of wheat and my talent for botany and spice trading. Slowly but steadily, I discovered the enjoyment of accumulation. Few pleasures in life could compare to being certain I wouldn't miss out on a hot meal or lack a roof over my head, that wealth could be multiplied, accumulation gave me power. I had also learned from my mistakes: since my house and life had been transparent for the reverend in Saugus, and my body a suspicious object to be monitored, only through the art of concealment would I survive in Salem.

Speaking of the first reverend, I'd been able to silence him with the Second Epistle to the Corinthians, but what was the point of deceiving this new one? Reverend Peter was much more powerful and intelligent and, therefore, much more dangerous. The fact that my house was near his was a problem, I will not deny it. Many would have been daunted. But I'd already learned that my age was an advantage, as was being a widow. We recognised each other at church, regardless of our age, or whether we were rich or poor, it didn't matter. We all knew what our options were and we diligently made the most of them. As women, we'd been confined to the household and the family, but what should become of us as widows? Many of us had already raised our children and they had started families of their own. Even my dear Henry had returned to Saugus and met a devout and dull girl whom he hoped to marry. He was a common blacksmith and well-adapted to the traditions of the New World.

Although it was difficult to part from Henry I felt that, somehow, it was time. Plus, our distance protected him from whatever else might happen, because in the New World inexplicable things occurred, frightening more sensitive souls. Not long after I'd moved into my new house I heard something strange: in Salem women disappeared. Not many, but they disappeared. They were usually young women, quiet and disciplined from good families, who, from one day to the next, vanished without a trace. Not even their kin could explain the inexplicable, all they could do was express their fear of God, like everyone else. The neighbours murmured at their doorsteps, at the entrance to the church, as if their whispering before a religious service could chase away a spirit with designs on us. People told me to be careful of the devil, they said Salem might seem safe but the devil was all around.

This new life was still filled with secrets. I could continue to buy and sell, but discreetly, without making a fuss. I couldn't speak in public or take part in politics. I couldn't even occupy myself with a family, although that had become irrelevant for me. Salem offered a clean slate to take advantage of, a blank canvas where I could paint my own future – albeit not according to my choosing, given that I had to follow a series of rules. Sin lurks at the doorstep, everyone said. Ah, but the founding fathers gave us the thinnest thread to unravel, without envisioning all the implications. How could they not have realised it? They left the domestic sphere to us women, along with the obligation to preach morals and religion amongst ourselves. Wasn't this a form of paradise? In Salem we could come and go as we pleased, from house to house, with the peace of mind that we were fulfilling the precepts of the community. We visited the sick, we supported the missions to evangelise savages. We could even teach your divine word (always behind closed doors and only for other women to hear). Our ceiling was low, but we had room to breathe.

Ten or fifteen women all in one house without the need to whisper, speaking and debating the word of God. Were those men all idiots? How could they not have realised it?

Anne. Now that it's all over, and since I'll never see her again, allow me, dear Lord, to remember everything that happened before the pain. The first time I saw her she was curing a wound on her young daughter's knee, a girl with hair the colour of red hot coals, our dear Susanna. Anne could do anything, her hands were like little birds, her skin like porcelain. She was somewhat younger than I, not much, but I always felt like she could have been my daughter. Or even better, a sharp and nimble niece with whom I had no blood relation. Blood, as we all know, leads to no good. We had both grown up in the countryside, I later found out, and spent the early part of our adult lives in London, at practically the same time. It was a miracle we hadn't met there, or perhaps the miracle was us meeting later on, in that blank slate we called Salem.

Now that time has passed and all that's left is this salty dust in my mouth, let me recall what I found so enchanting about her: it was her capacity to juggle it all, she was a wife with a dozen children, she ran a house, and, even so, she had the tenacity to abide by your divine plan. Nothing distracted Anne when she was focused on her calling, not even her husband, Mr Hutchinson, a quiet man who caused no trouble. Even on that front she had chosen well. Living as such is an art, and she did it stupendously well. She never complained of her duties; her sermons were incredibly accurate and intelligent. And besides, she knew she was educating her children to be part of a successful bloodline. Her older children were to prosper in our new Promised Land, and fate proved it to be true. What happened to the eldest? Did he become a general? A merchant? Oh, Lord, sometimes you play these tricks on me and my memory fails. But I do recall the most important part: her profession as a midwife in this new world gave her access to all the women we were going to convince to join our revolution. She was perfect, my Anne, just perfect.

Together we were grand, don't you think? Now, dear Lord, I'm haunted by the day we met, when we were in our prime. Almighty Father, do not make me speak of what came thereafter. Let me remember her just how we met, leave me *my* Anne for just one instant, just this moment, beneath this salty earth. In the end, we have all of eternity for everything else.

10. CARRER DEL CARME (BEFORE)

Three Pakistani brothers sprawl in three swivel chairs under the glowing lights of the internet café. It's eleven o'clock on an icy-cold morning in November and all three of them feel shiftless. They only opened ten minutes ago because of the girl I see now, reflected in the glass, who's been lurking outside for a while, unable to decide whether or not to go in, like a fickle cat – like the cats that wander around the Drassanes shipyard and the port stalking scraps of rotten fish left behind by seagulls. The seagulls keep getting bigger and fatter, any day now they'll be eating the cats, no one would think twice of it. Stranger and stranger things keep happening, the animals have become agitated. There's a city legend about a hole that connects to the underworld and this hole is supposedly located below the three chimneys of Sant Adrià del Besòs, those enormous blocks of concrete that look as if they came straight out of a science fiction film. But I don't believe it, I know the portal to the underworld is actually somewhere in the Raval. People from this neighbourhood have noticed the animals don't have enough space, they can't breathe in the dark and narrow streets, and lately they've been doing strange things. The other day I crossed paths with a dog head-butting a wall on Sant Vicenç street. I mentioned it to someone and they didn't believe me, but I know what I saw, and that blood-stained wall is proof, as if it were scribbled on the cement. Maybe the dog had rabies, but I'm not going to look any further into the matter. I wouldn't want to be taken for a lunatic.

Finally, the woman walks in. Her face is tired but her eyes are wide, as if she were trying to stay awake by forcing them open. She looks all around and asks for a phone booth. None of the three guys seem fazed, this neighbourhood is full of surprises. They assume she's just some foreign tourist whose phone has been robbed, or a junkie who doesn't know where she is, or perhaps she's both. Who knows. The woman with the tired face I see reflected in the phone booth of the internet café is, of course, me.

'Hello, can you hear me? Yes. You don't know who this is? Well, it's been a long time. Aren't you glad to hear from me? Sorry, I know it's the middle of the workday, but your secretary was so kind, she told me you had a few minutes. Okay, but you've got five minutes, don't you? No, don't worry, it's nothing serious. I'm all right. How are you? It's been so long since I've heard from you. Just today I was looking for your address because I have to go to Bristol for work, and I thought maybe you'd moved, I don't know. I don't know why but lately I've been thinking about the time we spent here together. I don't know, I just thought I could come visit you. It just seemed like it'd be nice, you know? I don't even have any pictures of you, now that everyone in the world has a mobile phone with a camera and all that. I was thinking about all the times I waited for you in that square, or you waited for me, and I bet we're in loads of pictures taken by tourists. I was thinking about all those elbows. Do you remember how we used to joke about all the photos we must've been in? That's what I remember, waiting for you in the square, always filled with people, and some Japanese tourist snapping pictures of us, you or me, part of our face, an eye or something. Every time we got up and left I knew once they were back home some slice of your chin or my hair or one of our sleeves would be captured forever in some corner of a photograph taken by a Japanese man, frozen there, forever.

'Anyway, I was just thinking that I could take a few days off and visit you. I think about you a lot. This summer we went to the beach – although he doesn't like the beach at all – but we went with some friends and the house was lovely. There were fig trees everywhere, you would have loved it. You'd wake up and open the window and there were all these trees heavy with fruit. We took a boat to get there, a motorboat, and the sea was really calm and blue and shimmery. When I was little I used to think the sparkles in the sea were glitter. Did I ever tell you that? Anyway, the thing is that we were at the beach and you came to mind because I saw a light-house, I know it's silly. It reminded me of the postcard of that lighthouse you sent me a couple weeks after you left and I wondered how you've been doing, whether it's cold there where you live… Of course it's cold, obviously, what kind of question is that?

'I wanted to ask what you think of people these days who put photos on social media, all the elbows and chins out there everywhere, over and over. It drives me nuts, not knowing what you think of it all. Sometimes I can't believe there's not even one picture of you and me together. Not one, nothing.

'How are your children? Have they started to talk yet? Oh, of course, what a stupid question. Nine and twelve? I can't believe it! It hasn't been more than two years since… It's been eight years already? Yes. Sorry. Of course, you're busy. I won't keep you long. Just one more thing. I just wanted to tell you that when I was at the beach I remembered that time we went to the sea together, and you told me I should do what I really wanted to do with my life, and I told you what I wanted was to be with you, by the sea, like we were right then, and you said that wasn't a real aspiration. You said I needed to seek out a sense of purpose, something to do. I can't stop thinking about that, and every time I see the sea I think about you, which, living in Barcelona, happens a lot. No, don't interrupt me. I'm sorry, I know I shouldn't have called, I just wanted to tell you that I've never stopped thinking about you. I'm happy, but I can't stop thinking about being with you. No, please, don't hang up. Really, I'm doing good, I know it's silly. Please, forgive me, just forget I ever called. Of course I'm all right. Are you all right? All I care about is that you're doing well. Sorry, I have to go now. We can catch up another day. Of course you should. You should come visit us in Barcelona with your kids, our house is so big. Thanks so much. Yes, really, there's nothing wrong. Goodbye, goodbye, bye.'

The three Pakistani brothers are wearing their headphones so they don't hear the woman there in the back, crying silently, holding onto a telephone. Five minutes later, two Swedish girls walk in and ask for a prepaid phone card and no one ever looks at her again. At me.

X. DEBORAH & ANNE IN THE MIDDLE OF THE NIGHT

I started this dialogue by speaking to you, dear Father, but now I must inevitably address you, Anne. What would I say if you stood here before me? First of all, that you were wrong, naturally. Here I am, talking to you with my body in agony but my conscience unscathed. How many debates did we have about life after death in your parlour? You insisted on discussing it with candour, as if it involved no dangers. You always had to go one step beyond, to the point of heresy, to war. I remember perfectly well how it all started, sitting around the mahogany table. You were surrounded by things, so many things, mountains of towels, sheets, fruit peelings. Taking care of one child or another, everything was chaos around you, but you didn't notice. In the middle of that chaos, or rather presiding over it, there you were, downplaying it. You pressed forward without thinking, like a sleepwalker, with the most profound conviction that all material things were a nuisance. Convincing me was all that mattered.

'You know better than anyone our love for God is a decision, Deborah. How can you fail to see that he has granted us choice so we can decide our own fate? Who decides when and how you go to the market? Is it God who propels you to come visit my house and have these conversations? No, it's through your own conviction.'

You could hear my silence, my doubt, like a betrayal.

'Who put you on that ship?' you insisted.

'God.'

That made you laugh. You always laughed with a hint of disdain when I wasn't able to see something as clearly as you could.

'My dear Deborah, don't you understand? You are the mistress of your own destiny. You boarded that ship with your son because you were poor, because if you hadn't you were going to die. I don't understand why you won't accept responsibility for your actions. You're such an intelligent woman! You got on that ship because it was what you had to do, not because God told you to. Not because it was "meant to be".'

Then my voice began to tremble. It was one thing to speak in private about our desires and thoughts, but this was different.

'But that's a sacrilege, Anne. We are followers of the Scriptures.'

'Of course.'

'Our fate has been sealed.'

And again, you laughed.

'No, Deborah. That's where you're wrong.'

You went on and on until it got dark outside, raising your voice louder and louder, trying to get this thick-skulled old lady to understand what we were capable of, who we really were.

'Tell me again about your conversation with the reverend from Saugus.'

'Anne, it's the middle of the night. It's cold and we've hardly slept. I'm frightened.'

'What are you scared of?'

'Of the devil.'

You laughed.

'Well, that's no minor concern. Go on, tell me again.'

'The reverend admonished me because I was earning money. He said I shouldn't accumulate wealth, and I disputed him by quoting the Corinthians.'

'And why did you do that?'

'What does it matter? I don't know, it just came out.'

'That's not true. Don't lie to me. Don't be stupid: between the two of us there's no need to feign innocence or false piety.' When you spoke your black eyes shone like marbles and you pointed your finger as white as plaster directly at me. Your tone became serious, 'Why did you do it?'

'I felt a voice urging me to do it and...'

You slapped the table with your open palm, causing the books on top to shake. A child sleeping on your bosom whined softly.

'NO!'

'A voice was telling me...'

'NO!'

The child's cries grew louder.

'All right!' I yelled.

And then, very slowly, as if a snake were hissing.

'It was my voice, it was me. I wanted to take a stand against him. I wanted to prevail over that pig-faced reverend who wouldn't leave me alone.'

And finally there was silence, Anne, and you looked at me with your tantalising smirk, smug from having won the game. Then you stroked my hand and hugged me, as if embracing a sister.

'Do you see now, dear? Can you see?'

I was quiet, glad to have pleased you, finally, happy that I'd resolved the riddle, even if this riddle involved a precipice so great, a leap into the air, into the utter, absolute void. But, Anne, on those nights we burned inside knowing that something was going to happen... There's nothing comparable to the anticipation we felt, the certainty that something would come to pass.

11. TURÓ DE MONTEROLS (NOW)

I wake up with a start because a rusalka has appeared before me. A rusalka, a demon. I think she comes to me in dreams, but I'm not sure because I hardly sleep. Perhaps she's there lying in wait, pressed between the glass walls of this penthouse apartment in the Castellana, and like a firefly, she only comes out at night. How does she breathe, if she even does? Either way, it doesn't matter. What difference does her material condition make? I only know that her appearance startled me at first. I peered at her from my bed, perplexed and sweaty. I didn't know what she was because she'd taken on the image of my best friend as a teenager, Victoria, a rather short girl with gap teeth, light chestnut hair and eyes the colour of seaweed, who I haven't seen in more than fifteen years.

Things I remember about Victoria, from within this glazed room, this air bubble of nothing: she liked New Age music, Japanese gardens and reading cheap philosophy. According to that description you'd think she was a bore, but that wasn't the case at all.

We met during our second week of classes at high school. Cliques had already been formed. There were the popular kids, the regular kids who just lived their lives, and then there were the losers without any friends, like me, who had made the transition from childhood to adolescence on their own and, having started at a new high school, we roamed around at recess like little lambs searching for a mother. Victoria was one of those kids who's so incredibly cool they can do whatever they like. She sat down next to me in a technical drawing class, asked to borrow my compass and inundated me with questions. Where are you from. What are you interested in.

Nobody had ever asked me about my interests before. It was such a sophisticated question, so adult, that I was speechless. Which was normal for me because I didn't talk very much. Ever since early childhood I'd found people my own age to be equal parts idiotic and cruel. I was an only child, so my parents had infused the house with overprotection and kindness. My socialisation outside of school started at the age of eight, when they took me to spend the afternoon at some neighbour's house who had children. The adults went off to the cinema and meanwhile the other children tied me to a chair and pretended to torture me with a knitting needle. I never told my parents anything, but I'll always remember the perspiration and prodding and, more than anything, that unfamiliar sensation in my stomach, a wave of nausea that rippled out to all my limbs, oozing like mud, as it dawned on me that someone much less intelligent could destroy me if they wanted to. The exterior world was an inhospitable place with absurd rules, teeming with savages. So I took refuge in myself and didn't trust a soul.

That is until Victoria showed up and asked me that question: what are you interested in. She said it in a soft, almost maternal voice. And she didn't walk away, even though I didn't answer her. I looked up into her lichen eyes and she looked back at me and smiled, and she didn't walk away. She knew how to see beyond my awkwardness, and she took me in. From then on, I didn't have to worry about anything. I had a friend.

Victoria's fashion was preppy, in dark polo shirts and jeans, probably to conceal her short legs and huge boobs, which made our classmates titter. As a result of those boobs and her sweet nature, she always had her pick of the boys. I remember one in particular, with kinky black hair and pale skin. He was a sweet boy who lived by the Vallcarca viaduct, near Victoria, and his electricity got cut off, because his parents hadn't been home for more than a month and had forgotten to pay the bill. Or at least that's what I'd heard. Later we found out the truth: his mother had taken off with the security deposit to pay her dealer so he wouldn't cut her throat. She was a junkie.

Victoria's mother wasn't a junkie, she was a dentist, and her father had left without a trace many years earlier. Victoria never mentioned him. Her mother had remarried so she had a younger half-brother and a stepfather who she sometimes called dad when everything was going well and they were all getting along. Victoria knew her family appreciated that, and pleasing others came naturally to her.

I smoked my first hash joint with her one day while the rest of her family was on a trip, I think they'd gone skiing. They left her home alone, which was fortunate but also clearly proved something we never discussed: Victoria had no supervision. She wasn't the only one. Soon I met several other teenagers with absent parents like Victoria's, or that nice boy who would show up at her house for a hot meal. Kids who did whatever they wanted day and night. On weekdays they spent their afternoons at the Vallcarca youth club drinking calimocho, cola spiked with red wine. Their heavy-metal bands practised at bars and they drank beer in the park past midnight. The ones with a motorbike earned what they could doing pizza deliveries. Pizzeria chains never ask how old you are. They were practically taking care of themselves by the age of fifteen.

Victoria's house was right at the intersection of República Argentina avenue and Gomis street, a ship prow of glass and cement from which you could see a large slice of sky and Hospital Militar avenue. There was a brothel on the ground floor of the building, and sometimes you had to sidestep a drunk who'd fallen asleep in the stairwell, his trousers still unbuttoned. But going there was worth it because of what awaited upstairs. It always smelled of Asian spices when you walked in. Victoria's mother practiced making dishes which she'd try out on us. They tasted a little like perfume and raisins. Food the colour of bright reds and oranges that stained the corners of your mouth, which we gulped down obediently just to be left in peace.

Her mother's husband appeared sometimes before dinner, sometimes afterwards. He'd smile at us and we'd smile back from Victoria's room. He lumbered around the house, clumsily aware of the fact that he was surrounded by burgeoning women who did things and had secrets and desires and whispered about it all. He'd just smile and shake his head, as if everything happening around him were the result of some uncharted magic.

In my memory, Victoria and her house by the Vallcarca viaduct embody the everyday colours of being a teen: café con leche, slate grey, and smoke from a joint. Victoria's responsibilities included walking down Hospital Militar avenue to the neighbourhood supermarket, where she did the weekly shopping for the whole family, and taking care of her younger brother. I accompanied her gladly, and we talked about anything and everything. The tedium of her routine, which she found so boring, was a joy for me. I finally had a friend, someone to cling to with the cement of teenage fondness, like a mollusc to a rock. I could finally escape from my own house: so normal, so sheltered, so dull.

Among the pine and eucalyptus trees on Turó de Monterols, Victoria taught me how to smoke together with a gang of grubby kids who went there every day. We would talk for hours, there and everywhere, in each other's presence or from home, where we spent hours on the telephone. What are you two talking about? our families asked, as the competent authority, amused or sometimes annoyed because they needed to use the phone. About everything *you* wouldn't dare, we taunted them.

Victoria thought differently from other people I knew, that's why I liked being with her. She understood how social relationships worked, which helped me to get over my extreme shyness. With her I learned the ground rules of the wider world, including the most basic among teenagers: you have to craft your own personal taste. What are you interested in? That had been her first question, and it had been straight out of an exam. She didn't care how people saw you on the outside, which was uncommon at that age. Victoria preferred for you to be unique, original. That's why she paid attention to unusual people. Because, in her own way, she was too. With her V-neck sweaters, her gold earrings and penny loafers, Victoria might as well have been a Martian at age sixteen, among our shaved heads and bleached hair, tracksuits and t-shirts of punk rock bands, but no one ever batted an eye. That's how much confidence she emanated. Her zone of influence included people who were unsociable, surly or extremely shy; she'd take them under her wing. We'd always been the outcasts at high school. The queers, the stoners, the orphan boys she invited to her house while her parents were out, people who confessed painfully intimate things to her that they'd never told anyone else. We'd show up in turns, never at the same time. We each had a singular, sophisticated, one-on-one relationship with her. Victoria didn't provide you with friendship: she offered you a secure, complete, airtight identity. She always had time and affection for everyone. Victoria was our Jesus Christ, to whom we went in procession, lining up at the Vallcarca viaduct or Turó de Monterols in search of kindness, day after day.

One afternoon I turned up without calling first and found her next to the empty lot on the corner outside her house, sitting atop a red Renault with Joel, a very tall skinhead who was in his third year of night school. He had his hand up her sweater and her face was flushed. I couldn't hear the panting but I could imagine it. I left before they could see me.

A few days before our university entrance exam Victoria called me at home, her voice trembling, and asked me to meet her in the park for a smoke. As soon as I saw her I was able to confirm what I had sensed over the phone: something serious was going on. She always bit her nails, but that day her fingers were raw to the bone and she kept trying to hide them under the sleeves of her shirt. Her foot tapped as if it had a life of its own, like an epileptic animal, a bird flapping its wings before dying.

'They're sending me to Brighton,' she said. 'My fucking bitch of a mother has been rummaging through my drawers and she found the hash, so they've decided to send me abroad. They say I need to focus.' Her eyes were wide and she started to nibble at one of her nails again. 'They're sending me off to be an au pair. Do you know what that is?'

I shook my head.

'Ironing clothes and cleaning up baby shit, that's what. They say it'll help me learn English. An entire year as a servant for some Brits.' Her eyes the colour of aquatic plants filled with tears and her nose started to run. I hugged her. Victoria cried and hiccupped inconsolably.

I wanted to ask more, but I didn't dare. I just hugged her for a long time and swore that I would move there with her, that I'd find a job, that everything would turn out fine. We drank beer and shots at the corner bar across from our school and walked together back to her house, the smell of curry wafting all the way from the lift. I didn't go in, nor did Victoria invite me. A couple of weeks later, after scheduling my visit, like always, I helped her pack up an enormous suitcase, almost as big as she was, before dragging it down the hallway to the foyer, under the attentive gaze of her family. We stayed up all night listening to music and chatting. Nobody at her house could stop us. I don't remember much else about that summer.

The next time we saw each other, one year later, Victoria's hair was darker and she wore a shiny stone in her nostril. 'It's a piercing,' she told me when we hugged. She smelled like cleaning products and Marlboro Menthol Lights and was working at a Spanish restaurant where, she explained, she earned twice as much in tips as she did in England taking care of babies and making beds. She told me what cunnilingus was, and that one of her coworkers had performed it on her the first time they'd hooked up. She was talkative and happy to see me, and there was something quick and decisive in her movements that I couldn't quite understand at the time, but I now know corresponds to being an adult. She also told me that she'd tried cocaine, and that it helped her to work faster and sleep less.

Now that I've forgotten everything, or almost everything, now that the pills have devoured my brain mass – or so I imagine, all that yellowish powder melting into my bloodstream, obliterating my imagination and my memories – only a few flashes of adolescence remain. I can hardly remember anything more recent, but I do remember being a teenager.

Like that time in our second year of high school that we went to some house in Comarruga with three other kids, and Victoria got so drunk on peach schnapps that she blacked out. When she regained consciousness she spent an entire day throwing up a mixture of spaghetti and water. There's Victoria, her hair a mess of damp clumps, as I hold her head over the toilet bowl, long before her hair had darkened from the lack of sun in England. Doesn't everyone know how to recognise the people they've chosen as family by the colour of their hair? The people you really know are the ones you've seen undergo a transformation, the ones you loved before they became who they are today, now that they've formed an identity more mature and less rough around the edges.

I know that Victoria's hair used to be dark blond before it became a mousy colour, in her twenties. I think about this now, delighted, from my glass tower. I remember one thread-bare rug that Victoria bought for her flat in London – I reluctantly came to terms with the fact that we wouldn't be living together – and how, when I went to visit her, we fell asleep on it after smoking and drinking cheap Spanish wine that we bought at a supermarket. By then she had started falling in love with boys she had nothing in common with. That year it was a Saudi with whom she and another six guys shared a flat. They'd embrace passionately whenever they crossed paths in the hallway, when no one else saw them. He wore white trainers and a gold watch, smoked marijuana openly, and one of the only times I spoke to him he told me that he wanted to be a rapper instead of taking over the family business worth millions. One day, very drunk, he explained that he had to get married to a girl with gel fingernails and iron-straightened hair from a good family – most importantly a Muslim family – whom he'd met at the Royal College of Arts, and who sometimes came around the flat. When he showed up holding hands with the girlfriend, Victoria took refuge in her room and didn't come out, not even to eat. Not even when I told her we'd better go take a walk. Victoria couldn't budge from that house. She started to read the Koran. She studied Arabic. She convinced herself that he was really in love with her. It went on for an entire year, until the Saudi went back to Riyadh.

There were more. A publicist who frequented the restaurant where she worked and who invited her aboard a boat that was moored on a canal in Camden; a Belgian photographer who we all knew was gay but – what a surprise – fell madly in love with Victoria, and she briefly converted him to heterosexuality. How proudly she strutted him about in front of us! Her man was perfect, or at least he was for a while. There was also a cocaine-addicted Italian skier who she chased after for a year, and who sometimes turned up at her house when he was broke or needed a place to crash. He'd whisper sweet nothings in her ear, they'd hole up together and she'd stop calling me for weeks until he left again. They all left, one by one. They left London but Victoria stayed, like so many people who get trapped in that kind of metropolis, like an insect beating its wings against a window. She, like so many others, worked at restaurants and shops in Zone 1 of the Tube while sharing a flat in Zone 5.

Victoria disappeared from my life more than fifteen years ago, right when she met the man who would become her husband: a kind, normal engineer from Valencia who offered her stability and a child. First they were lovers for more than two years until he left his wife and gave her what, I suppose, she most wanted. A family. Naturally, the end of our friendship coincided with that new chapter. We'd been talking about her affair over and over for weeks, until I grew weary. One night that she was going on about her amorous angst, I got fed up and railed against how long he was taking to leave his wife. I rubbed it in her face, how dependent she was on men and, to make matters worse, I counted how many of those humiliating moments she'd been through, perched atop my pristine moral superiority. I suppose I was trying to win her back, but I made a mistake. I didn't see the hardened lustre in Victoria's eyes. Nobody was going to burst her bubble this time. As soon as he made his choice, she stopped answering my calls and my letters. I don't know why I found it so hard to believe; she was entitled to start over again and, above all, deserved not to be judged. Victoria extracted me from her life as if she were cauterising a wound. She simply burned what was infected – which was us, our symbiotic relationship – and then she disappeared. The worst form of revenge, I learned then, is to leave someone hanging.

I saw Victoria again last night. She appeared as I tossed and turned, she showed up in my empty living room, as if walking on the surface of the sea, as smooth as a mirror. My rusalka, a ghost, a water demon in the shape of a woman whose disappearance, for whatever reason, was violent, without that being her wish. The rusalka: a siren from Slavic mythology who lives in the water. But I didn't have to resort to folklore to understand that Victoria was my rusalka. I tried standing up to get a good look at her, but something was blocking my path and I couldn't get any closer. When I looked down I saw that she had trouble walking, she was using crutches, and her legs were like two twigs. Her skin was the colour of rolling papers, transparent; her long hair, limp and coarse, like the bristles of a broom. And her eyes, which had been green and grey, were now entirely white, no pupils. Victoria approached me and, with her musty breath, told me that the boy was dead, that I should stop asking about him. Which boy? I yelled. And she simply smiled. Today, unable to sleep, I searched the internet for her until I was certain that Victoria is still alive. Yes, she is. She wasn't easy to find, she's always been somewhat slippery, but I located her in some pictures taken in her new neighbourhood in a Norwegian city, where her husband works as a consultant doing something technical and complicated. She has a house and a son and they look happy. Everyone looks happy in photographs.

After losing her I had other friends, but I never loved anyone quite the same way I'd loved Victoria. I still remember her teenage body, so dear to me. Even though my memory fails me now, I remember each and every mole on her arms and back. I know the colour of her unpainted chewed-down nails. I know what her belly's like, its exact curves. I know the texture of her skin when it's dry. I remember her white underwear, her bras that could hardly contain the fullness of her breasts. I could accurately draw the back of her legs, her body hair, so blond and transparent. Right now, in this empty glass house in Madrid, I can see her calves tense as she walks uphill on Hospital Militar avenue, scarcely a teen, tugging the shopping trolley behind her. I see her pulling it along, so heavy. I see her feet wearing old worn-out ballet flats, and I want to go back and help her carry the trolley up all those floors to her kitchen. Help her carry that monumental weight that she lugged along, day after day, at the age of sixteen.

Not long ago, I discovered that Turó de Monterols

doesn't exist. Its official name is 'Monterols Park.' When I was a teen it was just Turó de Monterols, the dirty steps where skinheads and pot smokers in tracksuits hung out while they skipped class.

On these sleepless nights I spend at the computer, I've realised by looking at the city council's website that the dirty 'hill' where I spent part of my adolescence is more than a cold stone staircase. Beyond it there is some sort of forest with oaks, cypresses and holm oaks, and there are swings for children. People now go there for a run and to walk their well-fed dogs from nice neighbourhoods, Sant Gervasi and Putxet. But the two of us never climbed that little hill. We never went beyond that staircase. It didn't occur to us to take a stroll around the park, what for? Our world was circumscribed by those stone steps and two flowerbeds filled with cigarette butts; we didn't need anything else.

The 'hill' is a park, Victoria's body is no longer, I'll never see it again. I'm sure of this now. I touch the glass of my cold window and make peace with the fact that Victoria has vanished from my life, but she's always here, if I turn around I can almost see her, like those steps from my past that no longer exist. Victoria, my ghost, my rusalka.

XI. DEBORAH, ANNE & THE WOMEN

When I think about it now, I'm surprised by how quickly I got over the strangeness of living in this new land. It didn't take me long to get used to the fishy smell of the port, the endless horizon of the sea, or the low-roofed houses that were much smaller but tremendously practical. From my raised plot on the outskirts of what had started to become a city, I contemplated the Bay every morning, letting my eyes take in everything that was ours, finally ours. And I started to sketch the map in my head.

By trading goods, accumulating lands and making loans to small businesses my finances had become increasingly stable. I was a woman, yes, but many men needed me: I loaned a small sum to a stableman to expand his business, another loan to the granary for a new roof. Thus, little by little, I positioned myself as indispensable. My widowhood seemed to protect me from the inquisitive gaze of the authorities, that is, the Church. Anne urged me not to be tempted by this lifestyle: 'Choose the employment or vocation in which you can be the most useful to God. Do not choose according to what will make you the wealthiest or most honourable, but rather where you can do the greatest good and avoid sin as much as possible.'

Sin? Me? A woman over the age of fifty a sinner? When it came down to it sometimes Anne surprised me. But she wasn't referring to my body as a form of temptation, rather to my increasingly evident comfort given my new position. I was tormented by these thoughts and I paced back and forth from one end of my house to the other, promising myself that my eyes wouldn't be dazzled by gold, that my heart wouldn't be bewitched by glory or the delight of earthly treasures. I thought of you, Lord, and I longed for your guidance not to fall into the temptation of prosperity, but instead attain a soul fortified by your grace.

Anne could read the anguish on my face each and every time. And it was she who rescued me: 'Come to the forest with me at sunset,' she whispered one day upon noticing that I was tired and uninspired.

So I followed her, naturally I followed. Anne carried a parcel on her back and wore boots for walking in the mud, and everything smelled of birch and beech, of cold air and wet leaves. We walked for a long time amidst the underbrush, weaving around bushes and arriving at forks in the road that she seemed to know well, because she chose the path to take without hesitation.

When night fell and my legs were pounding from the exertion, we arrived at a clearing in the woods where there was a small fire and a hut made from foliage and hides. What I saw from within the small opening in the hut's entrance turned me to stone. There was Regina Robinson, who had disappeared months before when she'd turned fourteen, without leaving a trace.

Regina was panting, covered in sweat, with a prominent belly and blood between her legs.

'No, no, no.'

'Deborah, don't just stand there!'

'No, no, no.'

'I need your help. A child is on the way and you must help me bring it into the world.'

I, who had not been frightened on the boat, who'd been unfazed by the rats and rot, now found myself unable to remain there. I left the hut and walked over to stand by the fire, covering my ears to muffle the cries of the Robinson girl. I tried to remember her a few months before, with her fire-coloured hair down to her shoulders, scampering along behind her mother on their way to church. But her voice was louder than anything I'd ever heard. It was like the howling of a beast, something guttural and unfamiliar I was forced to listen to as punishment for having attempted to neglect my own life for so long. There were still embers from the bonfire when Anne came out with pearls of sweat on her brow, her forearms covered in viscous blood, holding a small steaming bundle like a loaf of bread.

'Everything went well.'

'And Regina?'

'She's fine, too.'

The two of us stood looking at the newborn child, a tiny little animal devoid of consciousness, just a clump of flesh.

'How did she last so long out in the forest?'

'I've been coming to check on her every week. The Indians respect her because she's a redhead. They don't interfere with redheads because they believe they have supernatural powers.'

'You already knew that, didn't you? That's why you left her here.'

Anne looked down at what was left of the coals, or perhaps she saw something beyond them. Like always, it was hard to tell.

'Yes.'

She threw some bedsheets on top to finish putting them out and said, with a scowl on her face and a shadow of concern in her eye:

'Did I ever tell you what happened to my father?'

The question took me by surprise, at a time like this, so late in the day.

'No.'

'He was the one who educated me from the time I could barely even stand on my own two feet. He was disgusted by the lack of training the priests in our village had, they were unschooled men who scared the congregation with stories of the devil and didn't fulfil the word of God or his teachings. They were brutes who sought nothing more than a roof and some food in exchange for leading the service, which they'd memorised. They were real illiterates. One of them once accused my mother of giving birth to a goat. They only wanted to fill us with fear. Hence, my father tutored me himself, because he stayed at home. And just why was a man of his position at home? And not out working? Because they'd condemned him for heresy after complaining to the authorities about the lies those beasts were spreading. After everything we'd done! After the reform! We didn't abandon the Roman Catholic Church just to put up with those crooks as an authority, don't you agree?'

I couldn't see Anne's face, but I could hear her voice gushing forth like a flood in the darkness.

'He was put on trial at the cathedral in London. They condemned him to ten years in prison, where he fell ill and had to have one of his legs amputated. So he spent the rest of his life under house arrest. That's when I was born. He taught me to read, he taught me all about plants and animals. I am a midwife and a faithful follower of God's path thanks to him.'

We heard the howling of a wolf.

'We must leave here before daybreak.'

I nodded.

'But Deborah, please understand that I've chosen you because I know you have the tenacity to accompany me in this undertaking. You mustn't fall into doubt again, you cannot fail me. God is not out there waiting for you to decide whether to assist the women who need us. God is inside of you, helping you every day. He accompanies you but he does not decide for you. We've already discussed this several times. You owe this to him, and now you owe it to all of us. You must choose: join the cause, or I will not risk bringing you here again with me.'

Anne believed that those words were enough to convince me, but I was an old lady and a businesswoman. What she was proposing as a gift could also become a fatal trap: until then I had operated alone, with few risks and many more benefits. I wanted to help our women to become the mistresses of their own fate, but up to that point this had involved innocent conversations in safe settings. I'd always been on my own, able to weigh out my transgressions and save myself just in time from the inquisitive gaze of authority. Now that she'd taken me along with her, she had outright turned me into an accomplice.

Lord Almighty, dear Father, how could I not imagine her feverish eyes in the darkness? I understood that something must be surrendered in order to receive. How could I turn back when I was already standing at the edge of a cliff, propelled by that whirlwind of energy she embodied, asking me to jump. A companion, a collaborator, my peer, yes, my peer.

'I stand with you. I stand with God.'

I know that my words brought a smile to Anne's face. Finally, ever so slightly, a smile. Even though I couldn't see her face in the middle of the dark night, even though I couldn't see her, I knew she was smiling.

'Good, then let's go back home.'

12. PLAÇA DE JAUME SABARTÉS (BEFORE)

Naturally, you are on the verge of leaving me. I don't know it yet, because by now I've become a zombie and can only see what's right in front of my eyes, like a donkey in blinkers. But if I could stop and think, I would discover that all the clues are right under my nose.

We've stopped having sex, although that's not the most important thing – at least not for you, it never was, which still surprises me.

Things have started to turn sour. Our plans have started to lose momentum. All ideas for the Christmas holidays were quickly ruled out, one by one. Now it's February, and if I were capable of processing thoughts I would be able to sense that we won't make it to summer. Our things, all the many things we own, begin to fade. The photographs we hung, the books on the shelves, the sofa. Everything loses its colour and we blame it on the balcony. Who knew that the sunlight would slowly burn through our things, we say. What seemed like a good reason to be here, what we thought was a good idea, has ended up ruining our possessions, which is all we have in common by now. If I could actually focus,

I would realise that you are busier and busier, spending more and more time on the telephone and in front of the computer, in your office, which is now the living room table, where meetings and activities occur, where you come and go with hardly a glance at me. But I don't pay attention. I just watch time trickle on by, as if all this weren't happening to me. I spend more and more time on the sofa, as if I were just another object, and I move in and out of self-loathing. Take a look at yourself, I say. Move your ass, do something. The same thing happens to us. Our relationship has become that same disassociated photograph of myself that I can't seem to analyse, something that's happening to someone else.

Even so, some routines continue to endure. In this stint when everything around us is like a bone with no meat on it, I decide to proceed with caution. Since the day of our last argument, I've systematically tailored my actions so they don't upset you, although I don't seem to be any good at it. In the morning I squeeze some oranges just how you like and take the juice to you in bed. I'm careful to always use slippers inside the house so the sound of my steps doesn't bother you while you sleep. I don't accuse you of spending too much time outside the house. I did, not long ago. Somehow I've turned into that type of person. 'Where are you going this time?' I said one Saturday afternoon, sprawled out on the sofa again like a lifeless lump. Despite my general stupor, I could see a look of disdain come over your face immediately, it was so obvious! So I've promised myself I won't do that any more. Not now.

If I could see beyond my own nose, I would realise that you never ask me where I'm going any more. You're no longer jealous, when you really used to be – extremely so. Every man's name that I mentioned was an interrogation: 'Did you fuck that one? Really, you

didn't? You can tell me if you did, I won't get angry.'
And then, instead, a fight over something so trivial: a
shoe out of place, a teacup on the night table. But why
bother bringing it up now? You haven't felt like that in
so long, because I never go anywhere except from home
to work and work to home. I suppose you no longer
have to worry about it any more. When my family calls I
talk to them in monosyllables, yes, no, and my girlfriends
stopped calling a while ago. What's the point? I never
return their calls anyway. Work? It's no longer important.
My performance has taken a nosedive. My boss has
called me out several times. When I'm not in front of the
computer pretending to look at some document – always
the same one – I'm on the phone with you, standing
in the glass corridor that separates the communal office
space from the large windows that look out over the
shopping mall, wrapped up for hours in an argument
over some nonsense. My coworkers don't say anything as
I pace up and down the hallway. They're industrious, they
concentrate on their screens, they don't meddle in other
people's business. Sometimes, by the third or fourth call
of the day, I go and cry in the bathroom, but less and less.

The fights. They never end. But having fights means
that you're still here, I sometimes manage to articulate.
Even so, I've decided to change. I'm not going to get
into it with you again, nit-picking about how red wine
shouldn't be kept in the fridge, because that earned
me one of our greatest rows of all time. It was historic,
monumental. The wine. The wine! The safe spaces in our
house seem to be dwindling. It's a minefield and any
wrong move can turn into a three-day fight. And when
we aren't arguing, you're working – always, all the time.
You make long calls from the hallway in a low voice
while I eat cereal directly from the box, shutting myself
into the kitchen. My bulimia, latent at the beginning of

our relationship, is now a rampant monster. I eat things for no reason. Fried onion, fish pâté, an entire camembert cheese. I order enough home-delivery sushi for three people on the few days you don't work from home, now that you and your team are establishing the political party and they need you more than ever. I toss the leftovers in the neighbourhood bins so as not to give myself away. One day, one fine morning, you open the door to the kitchen and find me wolfing down an entire jar of maraschino cherries, and the look of disgust on your face is so horrific that all I can do is turn my back and spit the last one out, which shoots in a perfect arch and bounces off the kitchen sink. Nadia Comaneci, ten points.

Little by little, I sense that I would be better off transforming myself into something akin to a furry little pet, meek and accommodating. When you catch me at fault I work myself to the bone cleaning the house. I do the laundry, hang it up to dry, scour the surfaces and disinfect our things with cheap bleach every day, each and every day. I scrub the floors like I wipe away my guilt: too late, clumsily and enraged. I iron shirts, shake out blankets, sweep out dust bunnies and hairballs from under the furniture. One day your friends come over. You talk about the feminist potential of the new party and I serve you an aperitif.

That's the day when everything blows up, the day to which you will later refer. I don't realise it then, but that day will provide you with a pretext for what's to come. After setting out the food and listening to you all talk for a long time, I decide to get blind drunk on vermouth. Utterly blind. While you're discussing and organising the electoral lists by municipalities, I move on to red wine and my memory splinters. By dessert I'm so plastered I can barely distinguish colours. From what we've been able to reconstruct, it all starts with you asking me to make coffee. As it seems, according to the witnesses, I respond by saying that you should get up and make it yourself. Your smile, they'll later say, freezes, and you go into the kitchen. I laugh and tell your friends that you want us to have a child together but you can't get hard.

When I wake up, hours later, I'm lying in bed with my tongue stuck to the roof of my mouth and a sharp pain shooting from the nape of my neck to my temples, connected like a circuit. Your friends have left and it's dark outside. I can't make out the expression on your face when you ask me to join you in the living room. I do notice your self-control. Your voice is calm, slow and deliberate. Every word is measured. I've never felt so horror-stricken as I do at that moment. I think you're going to hit me, but that's not what I'm scared of. I notice a new tone in your voice, for the first time, as if it were a dog whistle, and it puts me on alert. There is no longer contempt or cruelty. It's as if you were speaking to a crowd at a public library event, as if you were talking to a pack of seventy-somethings waiting to get a book signed on the history of their neighbourhood and served hot chocolate afterward. You are no longer talking to me. It is then that I understand you don't *have* to hit me, I'm already dead. I finally comprehend the reason behind your pedantic tone: you are practising how you will recount all of this to everyone else. The most important thing is to make a good impression with that whole parade of future folks to whom you will tell our tale. As the adrenaline pumps through my limbs and I come to realise that no, you aren't going to hit me, I manage to make out something about how it's not working out between us and blah blah blah and it would be better if we split up and that you've already thought it through, because even though the rent is in my name we can change the name on the contract as, evidently, you will be the one keeping the flat.

XII. DEBORAH & THE THEREAFTER

I can only grasp the magnitude of what happened if I bear in mind what we did thereafter. Here, underground, I feel the same way I did when everything ended, when we were driven out of Salem. You condemned me to the life of a transient woman – me, a wife with a household, a girl who had been destined to be married off and chopped into pieces by one birth after another, like those women who Anne saved during our best years.

But, what about the thereafter? Nobody tells you how lonely survival will be as an old woman. No one wants to know anything about that. I've heard echoes, yes, voices, throughout this eternity here underground, echoes that my name was respected and even feared. Oh, Lord, the trials you put me through! The healer had spoken of an angel, but she never mentioned all the things that would happen thereafter, how they would deceive us, the miserable scum. How they would try to take everything away from me again. Do you think I speak about money too much? Allow me to contradict you. As women, we have been deprived of hearing about the importance of money for centuries now, the sole purpose of which is to ensure we depend upon it. It remains unnamed, and understood simply as the opposite of love. Don't think about money, they say, think about love. Oh, love. Our existence is full of lies like these. That's how it goes, I'm not afraid to say so from this imprisonment. Even if I'm dead I prefer to remember how I was able to save us. Because it's true, it was thanks to me.

Once the horror we lived through in Salem had ended, all that was left for me was the solitude of old age. The pacts. The grit of knowing the wickedness of men and being able to peddle alongside them. I had learned so much, now all I could do was start over again, somewhere else, one more time.

I remember our escape at midnight in a borrowed carriage, and the fear of being discovered, despite it all. I remember traveling night and day, flanked by two guardsmen who escorted us beyond the colony to avoid Indian encampments. Religious wars had been started, which were nothing more than wars over land, like always. Our governors took advantage of the tribes as they saw fit, making deals only to renege on them. Countless acres were burned with them inside, bodies piled up and then roasted, all to gain time and hollow out space. Evangelising is a very loose term that whitewashes many sins. Words, I'd finally come to understand based on my experience, conceal blood and horrors.

By then, I was tired of threats and death. I'd made up my mind, in the middle of that dark night, I wouldn't let myself be put through the same thing again. Long before, in that faraway cabin smelling of hides, the healer from my youth had spoken of an angel and of two crossings, but what was happening now was a slow and overwhelming torture. I wouldn't survive another trip, I had to settle down right away, and for good.

The voices came many years later, naturally. I went from being a dangerous woman to practically a saint.

They named a square after me. They said I'd been the first woman in the New World to found a colony, and it's true. None of that is a lie. I made a home for myself and ensured that no one would ever take it away from me again. I sketched out the streets on my small plot of land and marked where my home would be, straight lines at last, a perfect grid, the boundaries of my own little world. Better to know where they lie and stay within them. Is that an achievement? I don't think so, Father. It was only a practical exercise. A pact, in the end. Those were going to be the limits of my domains, and you know well that I'd earned them, I'd paid dearly for them. People had died to secure my freedom, but at last, based on pacts, I had my own house, safe from hazards.

Anne's a saint now, too, and I can't help but laugh. People are idiots. Only the cloak of time covers all us women who've suffered this ridiculous and inane glory, this sanctimonious glory. What good does it do us, once we're all dead? Don't *they* get a chance to enjoy glory and recognition while they're still alive? Isn't a woman who has been paid homage nothing more than a foolish guinea pig whose soft coat is stroked only after her neck has been snapped?

We were not saints, neither Anne nor myself. I hear the voices from above even though I'm underground, because I see and hear everything. I am your incarnation and your misfortune, Lord, and those voices say we were the ones to set an example. Us! I can't help but laugh, my mouth filling with salt and sand.

Anne would be proud, of course. Her undertaking was praised as almighty at last, albeit by merciless and immoral people with so little respect for God who are hardly devoted to following your word. If Anne knew that above this soil stand people who don't believe in you, I don't know what she would do. Probably rise from her tomb as if propelled by a spring, stand at the pedestal and start predicating your teachings. We all know that nothing could stop her when her time came, not even death.

When we arrived on this soil – yes, right here, because it was *this* soil and no other – after two starless nights, I was destroyed. I had survived, but could not forget everything I'd endured. Did I actually think they would let us get away with everything we'd done in Salem? I was foolish. I ignored the risks – *me*, normally so calculating and cunning. After Salem, the only thing left was to rest. After Salem, I had to forget it all and focus my hopes on a peaceful old age.

13. CARRER DE SANTA TERESA (BEFORE)

I'm killing time at a small, dark bar on Bonavista street that smells like a combination of hot griddle and coffee first thing in the morning. Through the clinking of the little spoons and the *pam pam pam* of the waiter knocking the used espresso grinds from the porta-filter, I can make out the voice of a woman speaking on the television. 'In the end, the EuroVegas Complex will not be built in El Prat as originally foreseen.' The haze that starts to settle in my brain is the same fog to cloak the Llobregat river on winter mornings. I remember that sometimes when we were in love we used to take walks around there and I would identify fish and birds, the reeds were flexible and green, the earth was damp and brown, a stream flowing out to the sea through properties partially overgrown by the vegetation. 'A few days ago the definitive site for the future megacomplex of resorts, casinos and conference centres was announced: it will finally find its home in Alcorcón, located just outside Madrid.'

And suddenly, the sea – yes, the sea – and all that sand and we were alone and it was windy, and it felt like the world was new and clean and ours alone. I remember, oh yes, I remember.

'The National High Court is seeking a three-year jail sentence for twenty participants in the siege on the Catalan Regional Parliament that took place June 15th, 2011…', the commentator continues, and I drift back into my head, to that time, and although I don't see you, I know you're out there making calls and organising assemblies and writing affidavits, and I can imagine the indignation and the frenzy. I know what frenzy feels like, precisely because it's gone. I know at some point I did feel it – energy that consumes space and time. I know frenzy is the will to live, and not this hollowed-out space between my eyes, '…as it deems they committed a crime against national institutions by preventing Members of Parliament from entering the building.'

I pay for my coffee and head out onto the street, on this weekday morning, walking as far as Santa Teresa street, just steps away from Diagonal avenue. I like Santa Teresa street because it feels like a mistake: it's right next to a big avenue, but it's a narrow bourgeois street with sophisticated, deserted shops called 'concept stores' that sell objects, I suppose, and fancy restaurants that only open two days a week. I instinctively scan for a rolled-down green metal shutter, but I can't find it. Perhaps I've mixed up the street and everything actually happened on Sant Agustí, one street over, I don't know. What I do know for sure is that it all happened late at night, the bar was called Ricks and I never arrived before four o'clock in the morning, after other bars had closed and we continued our pilgrimage to the spots that stayed open past the legal closing time: Ricks, Lady Godiva, the Black Hole. After the Black Hole there was nothing, admittedly, only defeat ensued, but Ricks was a proper, dignified place to get drunk. In my memory it has two floors, with sticky wooden tables and a long bar where a woman in her sixties whose name used to be Juan and then became Alejandra served us with a smile. The images of the bar are foggy, but one in particular remains clear: I'm in my twenties and I'm drinking beer with a friend. He's wearing a white undershirt and telling me not to worry, everything will turn out fine. I think it's because I hate my job, or perhaps I'm telling him about the Englishman, about his blond hair, his body. I'm not sure why, but for some reason the friend's words really calm me down. We drink three more beers and shoot the shit and drag everything out because nobody wants to go to sleep. We weigh our options until Alejandra kicks us out because it's already daybreak, and since we don't quite know which day it is I start my way back home to Hospital Clínic for lack of another alternative. I'm so tired and weak that all I can do is stumble downhill with the hopes of finding some water on my way. Like a wandering soul with a twisted spine, begging for handouts, I make my way down the street. I deserve to live, give me something, anything. Immersed in the dense shadows of alcohol and speed, all my senses heightened but eschewed, I watch myself become engulfed by a tide of humans, an enormous mass of people bursting with joy, swaying their hips. I see green and white leaflets, someone throws confetti and bits of shredded paper stick to my already scratchy tongue. I'm going to die, I'm going to die, I'm going to die, and suddenly, out of nowhere, twenty metres away I see an enormous truck lurching my way, the size of a howitzer, atop which rides Mayor Joan Clos wearing a yellow shirt clinging tightly to his belly. His sleeves are covered in something that looks like an outline of orange flames, and he sways clumsily from side to side, and I immediately sense that his clumsiness is phoney. I know it's all a lie, I don't know how but I know: the yellow shirt, the sweat, the swell of his belly, everything is a massive diversionary tactic, it's the false modesty of a pharaoh, that's what I think. Mayor Joan Clos will build our pyramids, I can see it in his eyes as he shakes some maracas, as he plays the lead role in this gigantic shell-game spectacle. Where's the ball? Where's the ball? And I burst into applause, bravo, sambalona, samba in Barcelona, sambalona, bravo, bravo!

Ten years later I am on that same street, no longer leaving Ricks. Instead I'm ringing the buzzer of a majestic building that has no doorman, but it does have some rose-filled vases in the vestibule, leading me to ask myself who changes the water. The lift takes me to the second floor, where a surly looking woman in her fifties opens the door.

I sit down where she gestures, next to a bookshelf. She takes out a grey notebook and pen.

'You called because you aren't feeling well.'

'No.'

'What's wrong?'

'I can't get out of bed.'

'Since when?'

'It's been several days now. I can't eat either. And I'm not sleeping. I don't know how long it's been since I can't sleep. I think around seven days. When I do fall asleep, I wake up immediately.'

'Why?'

'My boyfriend left me. He left me for someone else and now I can't sleep because I keep thinking they're here.'

'Here… where? In this building?'

'No, they're here, in this city. Everywhere.'

'But you know that's not true. They aren't everywhere.'

I don't know how to answer that.

'This sensation you have, does it keep you from sleeping?'

'Yes. I don't want to run into them.'

'I'll say it again for your sake: they aren't everywhere. Besides, Barcelona is big.'

I don't answer. Barcelona is as big as my cunt, I want to say, but I don't.

'You have to try to overcome this, the world isn't ending.'

No, it's not ending. She's right. I ask myself for the first time whether I loved you. What if I didn't love you? Wouldn't that resolve everything? I didn't love you, I force myself to think. And if I did love you, to all practical effects, it wouldn't matter much any more.

I don't tell the woman about the specks of light, ever more frequent, when I fix my gaze on any one thing. I don't tell her that when I close my eyes I can feel my temples throbbing, and that I've stopped showering, that my tongue is drier than the Monegros Desert sand at noon in August. I don't tell her that I see brown water everywhere, drowning us all.

'He told me he'd stay with me forever. That we would have children together.'

'People make plans when they're in a relationship. There's nothing wrong with that,' she smiles. She holds my gaze. She jots something down in the grey notebook.

'How long were you together?'

'I don't remember. Two years. Three? I need something for the anxiety. I need to sleep.'

Giving shape to this idea has drained me. I feel like a hunk of meat someone deposited on this beige, satin-upholstered Thonet chair where I'm somehow miraculously able to hold myself in a vertical position.

'You're going to take three of these a day. If you can, try skipping the one at noon because it will make you a little woozy. And I want you to come back and see me again next week. That will be one hundred euros.'

I give her the money and she gives me a signed

prescription. I go out on the street and feel the gentle spring air hit my face again. I walk by Ricks and my tears fall to the ground. I think it's because I've finally found the spot, but the bar no longer exists. In its place there's an all-night supermarket. Perhaps I should laugh, I look at the slip of paper from the woman with the notebook and think about how dealers used to see their customers almost exclusively at night and hardly ever, no — hardly ever on a street like this in the middle of the city.

XIII. DEBORAH &
THE GOLDEN ROOM

That's enough with all my circumlocutions. The mind sometimes works like this: one delays talking about a stretch of good fortune so as not to wear it out, even if those memories are one's only consolation. I have resisted thinking about the good times because I was later condemned to solitude, but it's time. Yes, now it's time.

We met on Tuesdays and Fridays at my house or at Anne's, during the day while the men were at work, so there were no obstacles, no need to give explanations. Anne had already earned a reputation for her gift preaching your word, her powers of persuasion, but once we saw her in action we began to realise, little by little, how great her magnetism was.

Women started to trickle in, I often encouraged them when we crossed paths at the market. They'd go out to buy honey, mint or some ointment, and from their uneasy and tired demeanour it was clear they needed support. They resembled mules, exhausted from so much coping in life. Most of them were married, but there were some single women who had been tossing and turning at night, asking themselves over and over when love would arrive, who would show up and make an honest woman of them. That's where I came in, playing the role of the wise old woman who listens and soothes consciences. I'd take them aside (staying in plain sight, no reason to let suspicions arise) and simply listen to them. They were like animals on the verge of collapse, in need of a stroke of good luck. Some had heard stories that kept them awake at night. For example, the one about Mary, so noble and wealthy, from the Massachusetts Bay. She had married after falling in love with a man from a good family, only to have him make off with everything no sooner had they departed for their honeymoon in England. When she arrived in London the poor thing had no dowry, no jewels and no clothes. She found herself in the worst of situations: pregnant from their wedding night with nowhere to go, forced to work in the worst of all trades, the one no one dared to name out loud. Which of us could resist imagining her, roaming around the foul port, a wayward woman, a bag of flesh and bones. Could something like that happen to me? asked a fearful young woman, practically pouncing on me in the middle of the street, unable to contain herself. And another who could no longer manage the burden of her eight children, her womb had been ravaged, her weathered skin was the texture of leather, despite having just turned thirty. 'Does God put me to these tests just to prove that I'm as good as condemned? That this burden is my punishment?' They were all haunted by this question, and it was no wonder: our community was destined to rule in your name, our fate had been sealed, and therefore all our actions, everything that happened to us, was a sign of your grace or your mortification.

We were consumed by these thoughts; uphill and downhill we dragged our heavy load, our uteruses on fire, such unbearable weight for all these women who were nothing more than animals in our colony, female beasts with a bit of reasoning. And it pushed them to the limit, they lost their minds. They were unhinged, their nerves were shot. They became the devil's workshop, allowing him to find the fissure and slip inside. They were like stones in the desert. But the devil is like water, that lone drop of water that trickles into a crack, day after day, until, turning to ice when night-time temperatures drop, the stone splits in two. And in the end there remains nothing but sand, tons and tons of sand.

Not to mention all the disappearances, naturally. All those young women who vanished without a trace.

All you had to do was go out on the street to see which ones would be our future sisters. Haggard, pallid and jittery like fawns. That was when I could thrust the sword in. Why don't you come to our Bible readings? We meet a couple times a week, surely you'll feel better if you come. Rebecca, Mary, Elizabeth. Sarah, Hannah, Miriam. Esther, Ruth, Belkis. Their husbands encouraged them – often out of real concern, or their fear of God. If their mules failed, who would do the hard work at home for them? Women were in short supply in the Bay, outnumbered by men.

And so, when they finally made up their minds and hesitantly arrived at my door, timid and cowering, they found Anne there to welcome them in with an embrace, her soft and deep voice telling them everything was going to be all right. She sat them down, like little white doves, and they gazed upon her, waiting for a spark to come, some sort of sign to make sense of so much distress, so much suffering. Why can't I go on, Anne? Tell me why. I'll go to hell for asking myself these questions. Who will love me? Why can't my husband calm my nerves? Why can't I sleep? It must be the devil, Anne, tell me the truth.

And Anne answered them, serenely, saying that God's instructions were clear if one truly listened. They had only to listen deep down inside, forget the orders from their husbands and the reverends, and feel their love for God from within. You feel it, sister, I know you feel it. Anne spoke of a place between the chest and the breastbone where all love and all yearning is found. From this place they could project the spiritual peace of mind they needed. She said their connection with God was direct, and that they could talk to you, Lord, and in their heart of hearts they would know which decisions to make. She had them close their eyes and with her soft words she repeated psalm after psalm, and as the wheat-coloured light cast through the window, my house became a big golden bubble filled by your word, resonating with the cries of all those women who needed your help. Having recited the psalms, often the same ones we heard at church said by Reverend Peter, Anne added some words of her own. She spoke of will and meaning, of the intuition of the spirit, and said softly that we, all of us, were actually operating from goodness. She took them by the hands and whispered: God will not punish you, Sarah, for being fearful of the future. You mustn't be afraid of salvation or condemnation, Miriam, if yesterday you lost a hair ribbon on your way walking home. That was not some sort of sign. Then Miriam cried and cried, and her tears could practically be heard as they slid down her cheeks and fell to the floor, such were the anguished sobs of our sisters seeking consolation. Sometimes I imagined all those tears gathering into a torrent and escaping under the door, out to Reverend Peter's house, down the street. We would fill that new Canaan with our salty water and turn it into the real land that had been promised to us. We were the ones who would inherit it, with the sweat of our brow, with the sparkling sweat we had exuded ourselves, daughters of the Lord, your daughters, those who truly revealed your word.

And the following week, we were no longer four but eight, and then we were fifteen, and then twenty-four. We had to look for a larger meeting space to be able to embody so much desire. Yes, Father, do not correct me: I said 'embody' and not 'contain' and I said it on purpose. It didn't take long before I realised our desire was uncontainable.

14. CARRER DEL JUDICI (BEFORE)

I know there's a jackknife open with the blade glistening on the glass table. I know it before I get out of bed. I can't see it, I can't open my eyes, but I know it's there next to the debris from the shipwreck: some strands of shag tobacco, bits of cardboard, a couple of glasses with cigarette butts floating in them, a CD case. If I keep my eyes closed long enough I'll be able to see all these things. It will happen sooner or later. I have to get up, I've been pretending to be asleep, but that wasn't sleep, that was something else. Being unconscious isn't sleeping. How long was I in that state? Shut down, turned off. An hour? Two, tops? And since then I've been pretending so I don't wake up the person lying next to me in bed.

I don't have to turn around to see what he looks like. I know exactly what he looks like: green eyes, long thin limbs, a huge grin when he opens his mouth and an earring in one lobe. I registered that face before my brain shut down. Another version of the Englishman.

'What are you doing in Barcelona? I'm here on tour. What do you do?' He spoke to me in English last night.

There's a jackknife there. I shift in bed and see some bruises on my legs and forearm. When I get up I hit my head on the roof. We're in a garret which, I realise right away, is a tourist apartment the boy with the green eyes has snagged for the two nights he's spending in the city. His fingernails shine while he sleeps, as if they'd been painted with nail polish, and I touch one. I'm overcome by tenderness, although I'm not exactly sure why. Still half asleep I do what I always do in the bed of a stranger. I search his phone – he has a girlfriend named Sasha in Vienna: *You ok babe? Call me when you wake up :)* I smell his clothes, I look for signs of what he's really like. I go through his wallet, I keep the two hundred euros he's got on him.

Ever since my boss called me into her office and instructed me to take a few days off work, I've been a little short on cash. I think about my boss, about the smirk on her face, her tortoiseshell glasses, her suit jacket. I tried to save us both from the unpleasant conversation, but I was unsuccessful. She said it would only be for a few days, but I knew that was a benevolent touch. The last one. As soon as I started taking the pills, I stopped going. What for? I didn't even file for sick leave, I didn't feel up to it. Since then I've been in an amniotic limbo that's not half-bad. The two hundred euros will come in handy.

Once, years ago when I still had an office to go to everyday and hadn't met you yet, I woke up in this same state in a room at the Hotel Majestic on Passeig de Gràcia. My guts were spinning from the booze and my face was mottled with red blotches (the guy I'd gone to bed with had insisted on slapping me while we fucked). I went down to the hotel bar holding my shoes in my hand. Gracefully, I ordered a macchiato. They charged me twelve euros.

Although I can't yet feel the headache I know is still to come, I'm certain last night was no good because my clothes are folded on a chair next to me. I didn't do that, he did. That means he fucked me and I don't remember. It's not the first time, of course. The gaps in my memory are increasingly frequent, more extensive and pronounced. And they all start at a bar.

Ever since you left me, once I'm able to go out at night again, all the men who approach at bars are too good-looking for me, like the bohemian fantasy of a Nordic furniture catalogue. They make their desire clear, explicitly so because they feel sure of themselves. They feel like they're doing me a favour. They open doors for me, they open their gorgeous green eyes too wide when I make a joke and laugh precisely at the punchline.

All these men have strange and curious professions. They're musicians, seasonal lifeguards, brokers from the City, mathematicians, astrophysicists. They're vegetarians, Jews, they speak of 'feminisms' in the plural tense and in English. 'Patriarchy', they say, instead of *el patriarcado*. They wear clothes made from natural fibres – linen, wool, cotton – and split their time living between Hong Kong and Berlin, New York and Jerusalem, Reykjavik and London, always cities characterised by rich and elusive worlds where they can devote themselves to whatever it is they do. They're all passing through. You should come visit, I'm sure that you'd be so successful in your field, they say without knowing exactly what it is I do. They all have flexible girlfriends who do yoga, jealous girlfriends, formal polyamorous girlfriends, racialised, thin, nervous girlfriends with long hair, who are good friends, who drink kombucha and are concerned about their intestinal flora, about the iodine levels in their blood. Sometimes they're there too, at the bar, and I get introduced to them. I'm not bothered. I know that their boyfriends – Uli, Andy, Patrick – will go home with me, and they know it too. I know it hurts, I think. I know it hurts. Sisterhood, they think.

At that instant, he wakes up and smiles. What luck. He scratches his head and pretends to be surprised by what happened. He says he'll invite me out to breakfast and I know it's to get me out of his flat, but there's something sweet and good-natured about the proposal. Suddenly, I'm less worried about not having used a condom. Or not remembering anything. I don't know what happened last night – I only remember my insistence on scoring speed at a doorway on Joaquín Costa street, on not fucking yet, on drinking more. I think I told him that I'd just split up and he feigned empathy. It's easy enough to tell the difference, you notice how they agree with everything you say – yes, yes, yes – just to hold their ground. And he hugged me, which was rather nice, and I cried. I told him that you used to hit me, which isn't true, but I was crying, and that justified my sobs, because I hadn't expected to cry; it surprised me too. I also told him the apocalypse was coming, we were all going to drown, and that he was lucky to live in a city that's well above sea level. After that I don't remember anything, but I sense he took me to bed and spread my legs and fucked me while I was unconscious.

The musician looks at me, expectantly. 'My treat', I say to him now, so he doesn't search for his wallet. I do the math: I'll have one hundred and ninety euros left to take a taxi back to the flat that, since you broke up with me, I've been sharing with a French student who's doing a master's at Esade Business School. Her father owns the flat. I plan to go home and veg out, flop myself down and rest all day long.

There's a jackknife on the glass table. I finally see myself in its reflection: swollen, rotten with guilt, my heart sick.

XIV. DEBORAH &
THE RIVER METAPHOR

We chose two of Anne's most fervent admirers to help us organise our meetings. My house had become too small, but luckily one devotee persuaded the governor to concede us the schoolyard. It was a brilliant idea: after all, our work was educational and making the move would further distance us from Reverend Peter's sharp and penetrating eyes. According to community standards we were doing no wrong, but our increasingly frequent meetings undoubtedly meant we had started to cross a line as brittle as the first frosts of winter.

I was in charge of notifying the women and deciding which topics would be addressed. Anne got up on a small platform and answered the most pressing questions of the devotees, who gathered concentrically around her to fit in the schoolyard. Anne turned in circles to be able to look them in the eye, one by one. The women's questions were endless, but Anne never became weary. She addressed the faithful until they were satisfied, and, as we had agreed, she used words that acted as seeds, planted inside of them. Both Anne and I were convinced they needed the right images to understand how much

God's love depended on their ability to comprehend willpower.

'Do not think, sisters, that I speak of free will,' she said in a soft and confident voice when the murmurs of doubt began to arise. 'What I mean to reveal is that we are free. We must be free to act according to our impulses and our desires. This is our obligation since our lives have already been determined. We cannot change our fate. We are women, God put us here to carry out the most valuable task of all, to give life, but we can also direct its flow.'

Then she fixed her eyes on one woman:

'Mary Robson, what has your husband Samuel been up to? I noticed that he built a dike along the banks of the stream that flows into the pond. Is that a sacrilege? Has he modified something in our Lord's design?' Mary Robson's cheeks flushed and she remained silent and unmoving, like a mouse who's been caught gnawing on a piece of stale bread. Anne squinted. 'Of course not, Mary, do not suffer. *According as he hath chosen us in him before the foundation of the world, that we should be holy and without blame before him in love,* Ephesians 1:4. Samuel simply made a decision that impacts the daily life of our community. We need those barricades to direct the flow of the stream, so that it doesn't run over, and to protect us during the rainy season. Isn't that true?'

All of them nodded, yes, yes, of course it's true.

Then Anne raised her voice. Until then her tone of voice had been calm, but now it grew strong and brilliant and shone with all the colours of the rainbow.

'We have the chance to act on behalf of the grace of God, because He knows that the intention behind our actions is nothing more than survival. The difference, sisters, our own peace of mind, is that we cannot act against fate, we cannot change it. Our actions show only

God's will to work in favour of the common good, not our individual freedom. This is why you must remain calm. We are daughters of fate, we are its heiresses!'

The women applauded, their eyes shiny, relieved and filled with hope, proud to have the best preacher on their side – not like the minster or Reverend Peter, who never paid attention to them, who stuck to the Scriptures and used the Bible like a crutch: straight, hard and entirely inflexible. Anne spoke to the women, she offered them a future and in exchange they granted her their faith, their time, their entire lives.

Afterwards, once everyone had left and only silence remained, we closed the schoolyard door behind us and set out to walk together along the path back home.

'Do you think it all made sense?'

'Perfectly, Anne.'

'And the metaphor about the river?'

'Absolutely. Much better than Reverend Peter's about the mirror from last Sunday. There's no reason to discourage them. If everything had already been written there would be nothing left to do.'

'Yes, you're right.'

Our words were sparing because we didn't feel the need to speak. We simply felt the wind on our face, and watched how the landscape changed from season to season. We emptied any thoughts from our head. Just between you and me, Lord, blessed Father of mine, can you believe how happy I was back then? I went so far as to think that Anne and I were capable of making the trees sway in the wind; Anne and I were in charge of telling you when it should rain and when the weather should cool down. What nonsense! Isn't that right, Lord?

15. PASEO DE LA CASTELLANA, 11 (NOW)

There are sunny days like this when I only find consolation in dead girls.

If the day is especially splendid, a cerulean blue sky, the pink and red flowers of Madrid, and giant trees with black branches that cool down Paseo del Prado, that's when, more than ever, I feel I must run home and seek refuge in their tales.

I don't look at corpses – I'm not one of those. I'm not interested in flesh. I only want to see photographs from when they were alive and healthy, gaze upon their aqueous eyes, their long and tangled hair, greenish blond in colour like a mermaid.

They're my dead mermaids.

The first is Anastasia, a Russian with an aristocratic name, cat eyes and a sharp nose. She threw herself off a building in Kyiv. In the months prior, she'd lost a lot of weight. From what I read in the press, she had recently broken up with a tall and dark businessman. They say she heard voices warning her not to be a coward. In the photos taken with him they look happy, they're the only ones in which she's smiling. Models rarely smile.

I contemplate the slanted eyes of Daul, her straight black mane, broad high cheekbones. In some pictures her mouth is slightly open, but in most she just shoots the camera a serious, sidelong glance. I find a video where she's wearing no makeup, taken with her telephone together with some other models. From her screen to mine comes the Daul from a few years ago, mock-interviewing a model with the face and body of a girl (she is, actually, a girl) admitting her worst fear: a shoe falling off on the catwalk and tripping. In one shot we see Daul with her nails painted black, her hair pulled up in a ponytail and her skin clean. Someone else records while she pages through a photo book and explains, enthusiastically, her love for Tolstoy. Laughing, she mentions that every time she talks about Tolstoy with an American they think she's referring to *Toy Story*. There's a break in the video and then it cuts to Daul in a hotel suite doing a silly dance to industrial techno music, wearing a dress with pink fringe. The dress is by Anna Sui, yells Daul. Her arms are so thin they look like twigs trembling to the tempo of a synthesiser. Her skin is a warm toasted colour and her eyes are jet black. She dyed her hair blond shortly after making this video and hanged herself in her Paris apartment.

Ruslana is the most notorious of them all. She's the one about whom there is the most information, more photographs, more everything. She had long silky hair; it was her hallmark at the agency that represented her, and her eyes were the same turquoise green as her friend Anastasia. Her lips were full, like those of a fairy tale princess. Her nickname was, precisely, Rapunzel. She was a model from Kazakhstan, discovered when she was barely fifteen years old in Almaty, her hometown. In her most famous image, Ruslana's hair is very long and wavy, her shoulders are bare and she's wearing a pearl-coloured tulle dress. She opens the doors of a sparkling castle and her eyes are wide, as if she's caught sight of an apparition. Over and over again I see that ad on the internet: Ruslana runs toward a mountain of apples and climbs it easily, with eyes like saucers, looking at something the spectator can't see, something off camera. When she gets to the top of the tottering pyramid of apples, her gaze continues to look off in the distance, lost in ecstasy. Finally, we see what she sees: a bottle of perfume in the shape of an apple that she carefully takes hold of, doing a balancing act, managing not to fall. Ruslana flung herself off the ninth floor of her apartment on Water Street, in the financial district of Manhattan, one June night in 2008. Her flat was two blocks from the river. From there you could see the far bank, the vegetation and the Brooklyn skyline.

But of them all, Lucy is the one I like to look at the most. Her face is perfect, as if chiselled by a knife. Her features are like polished stone, as if moulded from marble, sanded and shined to create a face rich in straight lines, curves drawn by a compass, three-dimensional mounds of velvet and alabaster. Her skin is translucent and pink, like Max Factor tone 32. Her nose is straight and her eyes are long and serpentine, as if drawn by a computer. Her eyelids are slightly hooded, giving the impression of drowsiness or, depending on how you look at it, unabashed sexuality. She is a model representation of the idea of woman: thick eyelashes, straight red hair, freckles all over her face, thin eyebrows arched in inter-rogation, her lips perpetually parted in a U-shaped smirk that reveals a pair of small and somewhat threatening incisors. Lucy is what the British call 'an English rose'.

There are many images of Lucy. Lucy sleeping, Lucy singing, Lucy at the premiere of her only three films. The stunning career of Lucy, the great promise of a body that likely smells of custard. A flawless, uncorrupted body, still unknown to the larger public.

Lucy had an argument with her boyfriend one night and hanged herself while he was sleeping in the adjacent room, between four and five o'clock in the morning, the hour of the wolf, the hour of woes, the hour of insomnia.

This is the hour when I search for information about them all, until dawn, and sleep never comes. I get into bed, but my eyes dry out, my throat tightens with dread and my legs flutter, as if they had a life of their own, as if they couldn't help but throw a tantrum. I don't sleep, but I'm not fully conscious either. It is in this state that my mermaids speak to me, right in the midst of this lethargy, and they tell me what happened to them, why they did it. They whisper the facts, fears that came true, immediate and final solutions. Their imagined voices become distorted, and they recite litany after litany. Their faces emerge like Ophelia's, obscured by the water of the black lake, surrounded by almond flowers, delphiniums, water lilies. Their frayed clothing is the same grey colour as their pupils. They are my returnees, my ghosts. As if they were bouquets of sea anemones, of precious jewels, I treasure them day after day. Their silence becomes imbued with words and I pursue my search for their pixelated flesh, back when they were alive, always alive, eternally beautiful only for me.

XV. DEBORAH & MR COTTON

One waning afternoon in winter, Anne's husband was waiting for us outside the school gates, after one of her best sermons, alongside a tall and thin man carrying a lantern. Anne smiled at them and turned to me to say, 'I asked them to wait for us and walk us back to your house so we can talk.'

I concealed my surprise and the four of us advanced in silence, just as the two of us normally did alone, until we reached to door to my house. I couldn't quite make out the face of the stranger walking with us until we entered the parlour and I started a fire in the hearth. He had a refined pale face and black hair. Although he must have been around my age, his eyes were youthful. They were the same dark colour as his hair. His face was worthy of a portrait, all his features seemed well-suited and denoted intelligence and cordiality. I boiled some water and served tea, which he thanked me for effusively. A kind man under my roof continued to be a surprise after what had seemed like an eternity in the Bay. That said, men had become increasingly kinder to me, this I'd already noticed. Ever since Anne had begun preaching at the schoolyard with me as her escort and benefactor, we had almost become notables, a pair of some standing. Something had happened, the consistency of the air was lighter, our steps quicker and more certain, everything was in our favour. Respectability is a tremendously comfortable cloak: it is invisible but once you try it on you cannot live without its warmth, without its protective veil.

Thence came men who were kind, an utter novelty for me. Gentlemen of all ages greeted me with a smile when we crossed paths in town. They asked my opinions on all types of topics, simply to have the pleasure of speaking with me. They wanted to be able to say that I, Deborah Moody, a pious and venerable woman, had shared my views with them.

Standing before me now was a quintessentially kind man who was diligent and somewhat quiet at first. Anne had made the introductions: he was John Cotton. His name was familiar because, beyond our own activities, we knew that alliances were being forged in the Bay. Despite living on the periphery, Boston was close and Cotton had already become a figure of certain importance there. At the time he called himself a rebel reformist, or something along those lines, at least that's what we'd heard in our town. Anne had never mentioned him and, in fact, I wasn't aware they knew each other. But she didn't hesitate to clarify, sitting between the two men and presiding over my table, with one man on either side and me across from her. They'd met in England. Shortly after being married, Anne and her husband had attended one of his sermons during their honeymoon. They had been so impressed that they'd become regulars at his church, which was a day and a half's journey away. Inclement weather was no obstacle: there were the Hutchinsons, every Sunday, to see Cotton preach. 'You have to hear him, Deborah, he knows exactly what we're after and he can help us. Our doctrines are one and the same. There's no one brighter or more intelligent than John. Introducing the two of you was essential.'

Cotton patted her hand lightly, as if to silence her praise, embarrassed. Anne sensed so and stopped speaking. Seeing Anne be silenced by a mere gesture gave me a shiver.

Finally, Cotton spoke. 'What my dear Mrs Hutchinson is trying to say with her exaggerated accolades is that the time has come for us to speak. I have been preaching in Boston all this time, but somewhat in secret. The governors of the Bay are not too fond of our shared belief that faith is the real measure for saving the soul. That's why I've been exchanging letters with Anne ever since we arrived in the New World. Women, as a group, are the perfect vehicle to advance our true philosophy on the love of God. Anne told me that I must meet you. She said you have a vision similar to ours. That you understand the direct relationship with God the same way we do, as a natural relationship, and by that I mean to refer to the natural world. How faith has the same components as a natural life: movement, nourishment, growth, reproduction and the expulsion of all that brings danger.'

Both Anne and her husband kept their eyes on him, all the while nodding as one does in church, like the women nodded at the schoolhouse, absorbed, thirsty for Anne's words.

'I understand, Mr Cotton, that you have come to congratulate us. There is no need. I'm overjoyed to hear that you share our notion of faith. You are welcome in this city and in my house whenever you wish.'

We all smiled, and Anne and Cotton exchanged a quick glance.

'That's not exactly what this is about, Deborah. The time has come for us to go one step further,' Anne said.

Her eyes shone brightly reflecting the fire from the hearth. 'John is seen as a nuisance in Boston. We think his sermons would be better received here.'

No, no, no, Anne. No. We're old dogs, Anne. No.

'But I don't understand. Do you really think that Reverend Peter will relinquish his post? I appreciate your optimism, but this sounds excessive. Peter would never give up his post to the first preacher who comes along, and least of all if they've caused some sort of problem in the Bay. Anne really admires you, Mr Cotton, but I don't see how I can be of help, sincerely.'

No.

Mr Cotton nodded nonchalantly, but suddenly his face seemed on alert. Anne and he looked at one another, they got up and walked over to the front door together. Anne's husband stayed sitting there, almost like a piece of furniture, which made me realise that the conversation had not yet ended. I looked at him, a poor man who had once been an honourable gentleman and now sat before me with hunched shoulders. I asked myself about the nature of their relationship. Did they still love one another as they had the day they'd met? Perhaps, despite my own failures, this was possible for others. Perhaps they'd achieved an understanding that had escaped me. Anne never discussed her husband with me, but they were expecting their fourteenth child. They were a couple who got on well, although at this particular moment, perhaps from the gleam of the fire, I noticed Mr Hutchinson's sunken cheeks and wondered if Anne wasn't somehow sucking the blood from him, consuming him. The guilt from having had such a macabre thought suddenly made my face flush with embarrassment. Luckily, no one noticed.

The firewood crackled as Anne and Cotton exchanged incomprehensible words and stood looking each other in the eye for a long and loaded moment, a strange moment between the two of them, during which I had to avert my gaze and instead looked straight ahead until it had finally ended.

Anne walked over and regarded me.

'We think it's time for men to join the struggle, for them to take part in our meetings,' she said. 'It's the only way we'll expand our faith.'

It was then that I sensed a heaviness in my chest, a scarlet wave of blood and mud, making my body feel like a dead weight. It was the culmination of everything I'd been uncapable of seeing until then. Everything I didn't want to accept, despite the fact that it was right under my nose.

'John is my teacher, Deborah. The words I've been preaching, day after day in my sermons, are *his* words.'

16. CARRER DE VERDI (BEFORE)

I'm sitting with a girlfriend at a bar on Verdi street when I realise that I am single. I know it, because I am detested by everything around me, and that's one of the bad things about being single: you have to do a bunch of things you detest. You have to do all the same things when you're in a relationship, but at least there's someone else along for the ride, someone you can despise because of all those things you have to do.

We're at a bar with a vile name, something like Cadaqués, Montblanc or Senyora Pepita. The waiters are two Ecuadorians who, with all the apathy they can muster, serve us l'Escala salt-cured anchovies and reheated Cerdanya *trinxat*. Sitting across from me is a thirty-eight-year-old woman drinking a beer and droning on about a man, and I realise I'm single again, there's no doubt about it.

Mind you, being single in and of itself is not the problem. If only it were so simple. From under my new haze of anxiolytics I can barely capture what's going on around me, but today it's crystal clear. Since I've just been dumped and I'm single again, I've made my way back to a ritual I'd forgotten all about: having to listen to another woman complain about a man. I look at her thin mouth, painted carmine, and it resembles a gash in the skin, opening and closing in an endless lament, like that of a Steppenwolf, a primitive lament, musical and repetitive, and I conclude that I am entirely fucked.

This is my penance. I have been so wicked I am doomed to repeat this scene, like Sisyphus's punishment, for all of eternity. Blathering friends who whine about men are my life-long sentence. They'll impose themselves upon me, one after another, in an assembly line until I collapse, exhausted. And again, the following day, over and over. The irony, I'll let you know, does not escape me, being that I'm high up to my eyebrows on benzodiazepines because I'm in exactly the same situation as they are. Oh no. But at least I don't want to see anybody. I don't speak. Incidentally, that is irrelevant: nobody needs me to speak. I've already realised this. My interlocutors couldn't care less. I could be made of papier-mâché, it wouldn't matter one bit. When you are capable of socialising in a practically vegetative state without anyone noticing it, you realise how little other people care. This dawns on me now in this never-ending moment in time, at this soporific soirée, this bar on Verdi street, this grey vein that traverses Barcelona's forearm from Gràcia to Vallcarca, this musical, semi-pedestrian river that serves to delight liberal and professional thirty-somethings on Saturday evenings, where they take a stroll with their children named Max, Leo, Jan, Lola, Candela. If, right now, I decided to get up from this bar and yell 'Max, Lola, time for dinner!' in the middle of Plaça de la Revolució, twenty-odd kids playing at the playground would jump off their red, yellow and blue swings and slides and obediently approach me in single file.

As I ponder the children, I admire the way the slit in my friend's mouth moves, and I nod. All I have to do is nod, that's enough. When I was with you I didn't have to socialise if I didn't want to, and I didn't have any reason to walk along Verdi street. I suppose that if you came back to me I could get away with never having to walk down Verdi street ever again, or do any of the other things I detest doing. But you're not coming back. Not now. Any sane person would tell me I can still get away without doing these things, but that's not true. Being single mandates you to abide by a series of indispensable rituals. Above all, you must maintain a minimal network of social relationships so you don't end up talking to an adjustable lamp or a plant or a blathering idiot. To seem like a normal person, you must endure certain situations – at least on weekends. And that's why you resign yourself to a stream of unbearable activities. Ethiopian food. Experimental music concerts. Going out with girlfriends.

That's right, girlfriends. Because *this* is about girlfriends. *This* is about salvaging the deep ties connecting you to a person you once had something in common with, someone you took pills with at a nightclub, someone who's perhaps met your parents. That's why I'm here now, at one of these abominable bars on Verdi street in the suffocating month of July. Yes, this is about girlfriends, like the one sitting across from me. This friend's parents had to go to great efforts so that their little girl, their only daughter, could be the first in the family to attend university. Naturally, she was able to choose her major, disregarding the years when her parents had to pinch pennies, take out loans and drink reheated coffee. So, did she opt for medicine or engineering? No, 'whatever our baby wants', said papa, so she chose humanities, and now she's a successful professional, the head of new multiplatform digital content at a multinational corporation. And, even so, she isn't happy. That is *her* sentence. So much effort, so much devotion, have made her believe she's some sort of genius who deserves it all. And her lack of accomplishment (can anyone really have it all?) means her resentment is immense. I can see her envy, I can smell it. She's about to flaunt it for the person sitting in front of her, that is, me.

This friend from my past hates me, I know it. I know because of various clues that are beside the point. The most important and defining one is that she's waited until now, now that I'm not doing well, to propose the two of us get together, and she's clearly taking pleasure in seeing me at my worst. This friend who's yapping away and who I've just got back is telling me stories about New York and London, and all about the salary she makes by doing something expensive and useless, something I don't know how to do, I don't even know what it means. She repeats her six-figure salary because she assumes I don't have a pot to piss in. She assumes correctly. This friend, who's so superior to me and speaks three languages fluently, has something to tell me. Of course she does: it's all about her entangled love life filled with martinis and effrontery, taxis at midnight, calls from Helsinki, sex at hotels. She speaks of acts that are foreign to me, as foreign as if a Bengali tiger were to show up at this bar on a Saturday night. This friend, who couldn't care less about me, demands that I answer her one thing and one thing only, the most important one: will he leave her? And my entire mission is, of course, to assure her that the fifth married man she's met in the last five years is going to leave his wife. That's why I'm here. I am a gutter rat. I am scum. This is why I'm on Verdi street sitting across from a thirty-eight-year-old woman with skin pampered by creams and treatments and who doesn't give a fuck about me. So that I can tell her yes. Of course. He's going to leave her.

My friend orders another beer and suddenly there's something in her hibiscus-coloured satin blouse that stabs me with an overwhelming sense of sadness. She goes on and on about their last rendezvous in Ljubljana or Istanbul while I begin to notice what's looming under the surface of her blood-coloured manicure, vitamin injections and starting-to-sag eyelids. I ask her to show me a picture of Frank, Gary or John and she shows me a very attractive, successful man with grey hair and dark eyes who's slim and well-dressed. Who is not going to leave his wife, who is the spitting image of someone with a peaceful life, who has subscriptions to foreign magazines and loves Chilean wine. I gather, from her expectant silence, that she is waiting for a reaction, something more than my face, which droops like a sack of potatoes due to the effect of the pills and is about to plummet on top of the plate of *trinxat*. Then I agree with something I didn't hear, I say yes, yes, of course, you're right. By her grimace of disappointment I sense this was the wrong response. I've said the wrong thing. I contemplate the line of sweat that's started to form beneath her absurdly expensive blouse and she says to me, 'See, in this photo he's sending me a message. I know he posted it for me. He's trying to tell me he's thinking about me. Do you see that Gino Paoli LP in the corner?' I search the photo for the record she's referring to. It's a screenshot she's taken from Twitter and I zoom in to see a grey rectangle the size of a fingernail.

'We both love Gino Paoli, he played it for me the first night we slept together,' she says without missing a beat. 'I know he's sending me hidden messages through social media.' Yet, I remain unfazed, I just nod and say yes, yes, of course, and stare at her well-hydrated thin lips, smothered in carmine, and I let her keep talking. I nod at the right moments while I consider whether, when we finish our beer, I'll be able to convince my friend to cut over to Vallfogona street, so that I never have to walk down Verdi ever again, but she says, 'Did I tell you what happened in Neukölln the last time we saw each other?' I can see the sparks in her eyes and I remember how one of her boyfriends demanded she get a Hollywood bikini wax, and I also remember that she used to give her housekeeper ('the girl', as she referred to that particular fifty-year-old Ukrainian woman) packages of cookies she didn't want any more, packs of Chiquilin biscuits and whole-wheat rusks that had already been opened, cheap bags of unfinished cereal that had been in her pantry for months. Here, these are for you, she would say with a smile of beatific kindness. Here, these are for you. She wears grey t-shirts to Pilates with expressions (in English) like 'FEMINISM', and she votes for the left and is in a food co-op, and I think to myself, I got what was coming to me, and it is at this moment and no other when I notice for the first time that I'm rising. I can see what we must look like from the outside: two women in their thirties, at a bar, holding two glasses of beer on a balmy Saturday night in summer, surrounded by young people on their way to having a really good time somewhere. And I rise a little bit more, just a little bit more, and I can see the entire bar, the neighbourhood swarming with activity, like a bunch of red ants exchanging messages in code, organising meals, destinies, other unknown lives removed from this one. There's something happening beyond this and it's right then, as she pronounces the word 'Taipei', that I know we are all going to die. It will be soon, nobody will get out of here alive.

XVI. DEBORAH & LOVE

You disrupt me, Father, by pulling me upwards. I don't know why you want me to emerge from underground now when it was you who put me here in the first place. Macerated in salt and sand, what an uncertain fate. I don't know why you are obliging me now. What force compels my body, inert but alive, to stir toward the light, inch by inch? Are you perhaps in need of a tête-à-tête? Do you want to sit me down at your throne or sit me on your knees? I don't understand, Father, why you're demanding this monologue from me. If there were ever a time for you to manifest in the flesh, this would be a particularly good moment, don't you think?

I know what you're trying to do, even if you haven't answered me directly through words. You're pulling me up to ensure I speak. This is your way of telling me I must keep talking. Haven't I spoken enough already? Isn't this more than I've ever told anyone else? And, above all, why now? At this particular moment?

You're clearly forcing me to relive what happened, over and over again. I know it's true, but I don't want to go. I've got used to being here, underground. I made my peace with being dead some time ago.

But Anne, my dear Anne. After Cotton came to town, what else could have happened? From my garden, with a view of the whole Bay and the port, I could see the two of you approach, two little industrious ants talking together in low voices, no longer proud as you and I had been when we walked through town, despite all odds. Instead, the two of you were a couple of old hunchbacks with a secret. Or just one, because that's what you were: one old person with two heads, a two-headed hydra that spread at a relentless pace in every direction, like a fire laying waste to fields of dry wheat. Naturally, this is my resentment speaking. But since when is resentment a lie? Wasn't this to be my version of the story? Well then, in my version the two of you were a monster that slithered down the streets undermining everything you and I had achieved. Men had a plan, they had the colony, and their plan involved chopping up the earth; but our plan would have been the future. The future itself!

No one in the colony seemed to realise the shift, not at first. I stayed close to you two, close enough to hear that what you'd been organising had started to yield results. There was talk among the inhabitants of Salem. Why do I say Salem? The entire Bay of Massachusetts knew your story! A pious woman who inspired fervour in the believers of our Lord Almighty's divine words. She who managed to extract the sweetest honey from these words, thereby giving people a reason to believe in salvation. Our new world needed an illusion, and you gave it to them. The houses where you preached filled up with people, you had more and more devotees, more work, more love.

Ah, love. I still think about love now. I couldn't compete with that love, none of us could, that much was clear. I could no longer stay ahead of you, Anne, you had escaped from me. How could I even try to penetrate the mind of a hydra when both heads, unpredictable as they were, thought and advanced in unison? How could I make you understand, Anne, that what Cotton proposed was a risk no one but you was willing to take. Yes, you, because deep down who could shake that maxim that love conquers all? That repulsive garbage hammered into us, that love would purify us and make us invincible. You, an intelligent woman, fell for it blindly, just as the rest of us believed blindly in you. That was the trap you'd fallen into; and the rage I felt when I figured it out made me scrape my knuckles against the walls of the houses in town. I couldn't believe that you had fallen for something like that. Love. I had crossed oceans to spare myself from death, my son and myself, but you had made your way here following a man. And you'd convinced your husband, you even convinced yourself, that it was out of devotion to God. Anne, what a disaster.

Once Cotton was in the picture, our plans for the women of the new Promised Land came to an end. We would no longer be going out to seek our land, far from those who had tried to impose their vision on our reality. My money was no longer sufficient for our shared project. Now nothing would bear fruit. Now we would not grow old together. Now we would not found our own colony. I'd already started making contacts for us to move some miles to the south, to New Netherland, all of us women together, hefting our bodies far from that tragic and lifeless bay that offered us nothing in the end. But then came Cotton, presenting you with the same shiny trinkets we had offered to the Indians. Yes, and you believed in him, because love conquers all, and one's word is sacred, and a pact is a pact, and all that poppycock that only stood to remind me of my lost youth, when I let myself shrivel up in the hopes of a wish coming true, holding on to that deep thirst I never felt again.

Did you feel it, Anne? Was it Cotton, on winter nights, who brought the gleam back in your eyes, the warmth in your chest, gave you back your will to live? I don't care that you're dead now, too. Answer me. What was it? His kind eyes? His deep and soothing voice? His truth? What made you abandon everything to trust in the eternal tranquillity of love? A tranquillity that no one, nowhere, has ever been able to attain. It most certainly wasn't your husband who pushed you into what came next. It had to have been Cotton, with his dark hair and voice of a beloved father. The father you regained after so many years of being an orphan, the one who was able to bring colour back to your cheeks and hailed you as a captain of the revolution that would never be ours. I suppose, because I can no longer imagine, only suppose, that the energy from a love like that makes one feel omnipotent. Merely having the chance to experience it must have been enough for you. But you abandoned us, Anne, just as our sanctimonious society had abandoned Regina in the middle of the forest where she gave birth alone. You left us without your salvation, without your word and without the chance for a future.

I curse you, Anne Hutchinson, centuries after your death, for what you did to us. I haven't forgiven you and I never will.

Is that what you wanted, Father? There you have it. Don't make me remember any more, don't make me keep remembering.

17. PASSEIG DE L'EXPOSICIÓ (BEFORE)

I hope she pays. This is the first thing I think as I begin to trudge up the narrow streets of Poble Sec. Since I no longer do anything except lay in bed or on the sofa, everything wears me out. Lately my days are on a loop, they've condensed into one single day. I take my pills. I drink water from the tap. I go for a walk around the block. My body has the metabolism of an eighty-five-year-old who teeters along cautiously so as not to trip and break a bone. Nothing inside it moves. Nothing stirs. The laws of thermodynamics have ceased to exist in my body. Sometimes the telephone rings and I never pick up. The girl from Esade who I live with, the one who owns the flat where I rent a room, has started to complain. Her parents, filthy rich Parisians who decided to invest in their daughter's education – something which, these days, basically breaks down to buying a flat in this city – are mildly irritated because I'm behind on rent. She, a twentysomething with milky skin and dove eyes who goes out to dance salsa at the Villa Olímpico, wasn't expecting a flatmate like me. I don't get out of bed, my room is a dumping site for clothes and pieces of fruit that I buy in my attempts to eat better, but which eventually decompose a few weeks later. I disappear for two or three days to go out drinking and fuck strangers, but then I don't tell her all the gritty details she wants to hear. She'd envisioned chummy conversations with a partner in crime walking around the Gothic Quarter drinking mojitos. She'd let her imagination run wild about sharing a flat in Barcelona, but I just shut myself away, leaving my room only to get some wine from the fridge and then go back to sleep. I don't embody the local dweller of this brilliant and bohemian city she'd imagined, and the truth is I feel bad for her. Because she's right. She deserves something better. She deserves strolls around Barceloneta and someone to listen to her. She deserves to be introduced to the good bars in Poble Sec and to meet loquacious young women with whom to form a posse. But I don't do anything. Literally. 'You don't even wash your sheets, your room stinks,' she says sometimes in disgust. I nod distractedly, apologise and pay rent erratically, in the hopes that she'll disregard my blunders. I know she's right. I also know I won't last there much longer. If she's patient she'll put up with me for another three weeks, at most, and then she'll kick me out.

But now, when I finally get to Passeig de l'Exposició, I'm pleased to feel the change in temperature when the winding street opens up. The morning is windy and fresh, much cooler than usual during this dreadful summer, but I'm glad, it will wake me up. I turn my face into the wind, until my eyes run with tears and my nose starts to drip. I'm a little restless, I don't quite know why. I look around to try and distract myself. I remember having read in some city council plan that this was, historically, an area with quarries and shanties, a space that was urbanised at random, departing from the organised map to which I am accustomed. Houses popped up like mushrooms; one century ago the power plant was located at the foot of the mountain, and the neighbourhood's name comes from its lack of natural water. *Un poble sec*, a dry town. No civilisation can exist without the flow of water, and lawless territories are always spaces of dispute, this I know, and it makes me nervous. Where there is no water there is no life, where there is no water nothing will bear fruit. Besides, at this point I can only think about the brown flood rising to cover us all. I wait, how much longer? It can't be too much longer now. No, it won't be much longer until it all ends.

When I reach a curve in the street, the smell of sautéed food filling the air wafts toward me, and my stomach contracts. I'm blinded by hunger.

Seriously, I hope she pays.

I've made lunch plans to meet up with a friend of a friend who's going to offer me a job. I got an email from her a few days ago, and I cling to this, as if Christmas were coming early this year, as if it could snap me out of my lethargy. Ever since you kicked me out of the flat and I stopped showing up at the office, I'm short on cash, naturally. I guess I could ask my parents for a loan, but they're on holiday, far from here, and that would involve giving them some sort of explanation about why we broke up. Considering how much my mum liked you, it would be quite a disappointment. I suppose I could go back to the city council if I really made an effort. There have been cases of job desertion much more absurd than mine, which were still able to rely on the magnanimity of our reinforced concrete office building in Glòries. I guess I could go back, like a wayward puppy dog who's been cut some slack for its extravagances, having now returned home for food. It's obvious that what's happening to me is some sort of a sign to make a change and I must confront it now no matter what. I have to strip myself from my previous life, renew myself. I have the opportunity to become someone else and the chance is now, it's been served up to me. I need to get a job as soon as possible, and this is the lucky ticket I've been waiting for.

I'm mulling all this over when I arrive at the restaurant chosen by the other woman: a small and charming space filled with waxed wood surfaces and low lights that's popular among the actors and actresses who work at a nearby theatre. A hip spot. A suitable place for a job interview for a woman aspiring toward a better future but not overly ambitious, I think, although I can barely think because my stomach is growling by the time I reach the door.

Even though I arrive early, she's already there, at the only table occupied. She's a petite brunette with light skin and a friendly smile. She seems nervous or energetic, I really don't know but I sense it's a mixture of both. When she sees me, she gestures quickly for me to sit down across from her. We're alone, it's early, and at this time of day the only other sounds are from people bustling around in the kitchen. Some dishes being washed, the clinking of glasses. From afar, I can hear the voices of the workers in the back, unloading boxes. My lunch date holds up a hand with a smile to flag down the waiter, who approaches with haste and tells us the specials of the day. Everything is resolved quickly. Luckily she orders for both of us, relieving me from yet another nuisance: lamb couscous and a bottle of white wine. When I tell her I don't drink, she just smiles. It's her first reaction to something I've said. Well, actually, it's the first time I've opened my mouth. Something in her expression raises a red flag inside of me, somewhere in my solar plexus, an unfamiliar anxiety. Something that would have been pure intuition in the past.

'This isn't a work interview, is it?'

She sighs and smiles.

'No, not at all. I didn't know if you would agree to come unless I made up some sort of excuse.'

As I hear her words I immediately lose my appetite, so when they bring us our food I choose to play with my couscous. Meanwhile, she eats and drinks with pleasure. She brings her glass to her lips and I watch as the pale yellow, almost transparent liquid disappears in one gulp. It must be a fine, aromatic wine, which makes my mouth water instantaneously even though I wish it didn't. Suddenly, a surge of oxygen makes its way into my brain and I sense something, something related to this place. It's a workday, isn't it? What day is it?

'I asked you here today because I've always liked you. I consider you to be an intelligent person, someone who's capable. If you had wanted, you could have secured yourself a good spot in the organisation. But we all know that sometimes things get... messy.'

It's a Monday in August, fuck. There's no one working at the theatre today. That's why the restaurant is empty.

'Everything's happening so quickly, as I'm sure you know, since you read the press, right? Well, the thing is that I'm going to be named secretary of the organisation and... he –' she doesn't dare to say his name. She must be scared that I'll get up and leave. But it's Monday. Maybe she's concerned that I'll make a scene, even if the only people here to witness it are the wait staff – 'he's going to be the candidate.'

Somewhere in the world, at this very moment, a child is being born. At the precise instant she pronounces this phrase a blanket of algae covers the coast of Ireland and a cow is being slaughtered, right now. I can smell the waxy vernix caseosa protecting the baby. I can smell the salt causing the fleshy pulp of the algae to crack. I can smell the hot blood flowing through the beast's veins.

'I think I am going to have some wine after all,' I manage to say, and she gestures for another glass, which she fills for me.

'That's why I asked you here.' She inhales, like someone who has to deal with a tedious task that she wasn't counting on. Scraping mud from a shoe, removing an oil stain from the cuff of a shirt. 'You need to stop saying all the things you've been going around saying. You know what I'm referring to. It could ruin us. Besides, what happened between the two of you is a private matter. It's over now, nobody cares.'

There's an uncomfortable silence, more uncomfortable than ever.

'We know that you've followed him.'

'Only once.'

She looks at me, maintaining the same composure as when she first started to speak. Her tone has stayed the same this whole time. She'll be a good secretary for the organisation, by all means.

'That's not true,' she smiles. 'Never mind. It's just us two women here, you don't have to explain yourself. What's done is done. But you do have to stop doing it.' She pauses. 'And you have to stop saying the things you've been going around saying.'

'I haven't said anything.'

'Well, that's not entirely true. You called...' she consults her notes in a little diary I hadn't noticed before, lying on the table in front of her. '...Monica, from the commission on feminisms, to tell her about your case. We don't entirely understand why. Whatever happened between the two of you is a private matter.'

'Yes, you've said that twice.'

We regard each other in silence.

'Look, I don't want to get mixed up in matters of the heart, but this is for your own good.'

'My own good?' I laugh.

For the first time I see her face change. Her gaze hardens. She asks the waiter to clear the table and she leans in toward me.

'Okay, I'll admit he's an opportunist, and probably a son of a bitch, too. But he's a smart son of a bitch and he's moved up the ladder quickly. What can I say, I'm stuck with him on my list of candidates. My hands are tied. I know you have messages from him that would roast us all alive before we even got as far as the municipal elections, and I want them to disappear. Otherwise, if the estimates from the polls are right and we win, I'll make sure that you never work at the city council or any private company over the next four years. Eight, if we don't fuck up too much and somehow manage to win the autonomous community elections. Do I make myself clear? Or do you need me to draw you a picture?'

I can feel something shatter inside of me, I don't know, something miniscule near my temple. I can't recall our life together or your face. I don't even remember your name when I ask the next question, out of breath, out of strength.

'So what do you propose?'

She smiles. From the window I can see rosemary bushes growing, here, right on the hillside of Montjuic. It's especially rich in plant species, both native (stone pine, carob, holly oak...) and exotic (jacaranda, prickly pear, agave...). There are also some deciduous trees, such as the cockspur coral tree from Jujuy, used in urban gardening because of its shade and spectacular flowers; and the fig tree, which is so rustic and resistant.

She finally spits out a figure. Some specks of dust hang suspended in the air, pierced by the golden early afternoon light.

'Double that and I'll leave the city this very week,' I tell her.

XVII. DEBORAH, MARGARET &
THE WATER

I got the news at daybreak. She'd been found on the banks of the dyke that Samuel Robson built, dressed in a whitish nightgown made almost transparent by the effect of the water. She was soaked through; her husband and some others had brought blankets to warm her up. She refused to move, she wouldn't budge, not even the strength of three men could tear her away. At first, no one understood what she was murmuring. It was Margaret Johnsom, Isaac's wife. She had never been to our sermons while they were still ours – just us women – but we did see her at church every Sunday, as did the rest of the community.

The Johnsoms seemed happy; and in fact, they were. We crossed paths with them on the streets in town. They were always together, them and their five children lined up like five little ducklings behind proud parents. They shared the bond of love. I think that Margaret kept insisting on this when the authorities arrived, there were no signs of violence on her body. Margaret hadn't fled to the river to escape from her husband.

Isaac Johnsom had embraced his wife, there in the middle of the night, despite everything, and tried to offer her consolation for what she had just done. I think he realised that the sheriffs would be taking her away soon and he wanted to hold her in his arms one last time. I thought about them when I got the news. The warm bed they shared, that fierce desire I'd known myself so many years before, fulfilled at last and then transformed into something else, something calmer, warmer and more long-lasting. Then, shortly thereafter, someone told me their relationship had always been like that: gentle, like the passing of the seasons, and no one could have foreseen what Margaret had done.

'A pious woman possessed by the devil,' someone said, and I felt a pang in my side. I remembered Margaret at service, attentive and reserved, a woman devoted to her husband and to your mandates, Father. She was a regular woman, not a fanatic. Margaret prepared meals and did the housekeeping, but she wasn't particularly overworked or on edge. She was shy, that's true, somewhat distant, but nothing out of the ordinary for a peaceful and home-loving woman like herself, making it hard for me to accept such a cruel interpretation. Margaret didn't go to meetings that were suspicious of heresy, she was simply a normal, everyday woman from town. Had Margaret been tempted by the devil? A buffalo turning up in the middle of Sunday service would have made more sense.

Even so, when they found her, there in the middle of the night, Margaret was not herself. Her long hair was dark and matted like the green algae that formed on the banks of the river, washed ashore like thick vines adrift. She was speaking to herself, her hands shook and she whispered verses about the land of Moriah, the land of Moriah. The simplest way to interpret it was diabolic possession.

The fact that Margaret had drowned her young daughter Nora in the river shook the entire community.

There lay her little body next to Margaret, she didn't hide it. Isaac Johnsom embraced his wife and people couldn't believe it. The fishmonger told me the following day at the market, in a barely audible voice, 'He didn't scorn her, he didn't curse her. He just took her in his arms in consolation.'

That story spread like wildfire in a town shocked by the dreadfulness of the crime and her husband's reaction, and it became a stumbling block in the path of many, too unpleasant to ignore. Especially when her case went to trial and we watched the Johnsoms, more serene than ever, more at peace with themselves than anyone had ever seen. After a few months in prison, Margaret Johnsom was hardly worse for the wear and she hadn't lost her appetite or her will to live. When she was questioned about why she had killed her daughter Nora, she explained herself accordingly: 'I couldn't keep living with the uncertainty that my actions could represent either my salvation or my condemnation. I wanted to know the truth, and I wanted to know it now.' There wasn't much else for her to say. Margaret had drowned her daughter to know for certain that she would go to hell. Her husband nodded calmly, taking her by the hand as soon as the guard would allow him to. I looked at her face, which I'd seen so many times on the street, and, unlike other people, I wasn't scared of her. I wasn't even frightened by what would happen to her. I saw the calm in her face, her thirst had finally been quenched. Margaret was no longer a woman who feared you, dear Lord, instead she'd decided to make you an offering. She was a woman compelled to follow a straight path, whose love for her husband and for your word never strayed. Her only desire was to stop tormenting herself with questions.

Once the trial had been settled and she was condemned to death no one spoke further of her. Not even Anne or Cotton. Margaret didn't serve anyone as an example. Her choice was an obstacle in the path for preaching your gospel and our chance at salvation. Anne did not once mention Margaret in her crowded sermons. Instead, she became more and more enlivened, and therefore more confident in her actions under Cotton's attentive gaze. From then on, she did abide by the laws of the community, like everyone else. Margaret became an unspeakable mistake, the result of an unpleasant combination of flesh and blood, another test you put us through to forge ahead, as long as we played by the rules. But Margaret, yes, Margaret, in her nightgown tinged grey by the dirty water, Margaret on the river bank. I tell the tale today not because it matters what happened to her thereafter; what's important is to never forget that Margaret existed. Yes, Margaret existed because I remember her.

18. PLAÇA DE LA VIRREINA
(BEFORE)

Naturally, as I pack my suitcase to leave, things happen.
Certain things always end up happening.

For example, a woman with long blond hair who
can't be more than thirty, or should I refer to her as a
girl? She's in a tank top and tight jeans and dancing with
her back up against you at a concert. The camera swivels
at an awkward angle, attempting to include the whole
audience and performance by a guy with sideburns and
a guitar who strikes me as familiar. I must have seen him
before at another show, back when I still went out, before
I met you. He's the type who says something cliché
between every song, but he says these things severely and
smugly, with the authority that a man from our gener-
ation who's up on stage can get away with: authority
times three hundred, stupendous authority, premium
authority.

Sitting on my suitcase, on my last night in town,
I follow the erratic motion of the camera, a stupid
contraption moved by the stupid wrist of one of our
friends who recorded the video that I'm watching, and
which someone else published on Instagram. I press play

with my thumb, over and over, watching the video on repeat so as to capture all the details in action. The scene is difficult to read because the cameraperson stubbornly filmed the concert and the audience, instead of you, and therefore the shot is basically a 180-degree pan back and forth, but everything I needed to know is right there: I see another friend in common, yes, our friend, one who I don't see any more because it's not true that friends can be shared after a break-up, he ended up on your side. His short black hair, bovine laughter and excitement briefly conceal the image I'm looking for. His brow is lined with pearls of sweat and his incisors gleam in a grimace of glee meant to demonstrate precisely that: glee. I recall – why not – other times when we all went out to similar concerts together. He's an architect on the dole. Now he studies Gestalt therapy. He has a boyfriend who's a dog trainer in Vallvidrera. They have a vast collection of vinyls. Then, as if everything comes back in one salty wave, I suddenly remember the two of them at concerts. I can taste the exact flavour of the beer from Sidecar. The shots. He always treated. He always had the imperious need to be enjoying himself more than anyone else, to prove to us that he was living life more fully than the rest of us, with enough energy to disguise his empty, smooth and spotless brain, like the inside of a Tupperware container.

The camera moves on, leaving him and his boyfriend behind, and settles on a group right in front of them. I see the orange lights of night-time giving an almost phosphorescent hue to the church in the background, the one behind the concert. It's Plaça de la Virreina, of course. By the way they hold themselves, it's clear they all went to the gig together. Like a school of fish they advance and recede, moving to the beat of some music that I can't hear. It's the neighbourhood festival of Gràcia, I can tell by the date. The festival of Gràcia means mojitos, plastic cups and feet splattered with dirty water, Astúrias street heaving with people queued up to buy booze at the kwik-e-marts. Perhaps later you'll all walk around to visit the stages at the alternative party, have a beer at some CUP-ster wine bar. That's how you and I used to refer in jest to the Gràcia hipsters who vote for the far-left CUP party, remember? Although I'm convinced you'll stay outside this time because you're not stupid, you know better than to be seen in a bar like that any more. I hit the 'watch again' arrow, scrolling back and forth through the video. You dance, letting yourself go, your face is beaming, and the girl with the extremely long blond hair, tank top and white bra who I don't recognise smiles with her back to you, without looking at you, as she sways her hips near the fly of your jeans in an intimate movement, joyous, unconcerned and happy. I get it. From within my sublet room on my last night in town I look through the glass but I don't feel how hot it is outside. I shiver. I'm cold. I don't go to the summer festivals. I watch the airplanes fly by, slicing the sky in two, and I imagine you and the blonde with the healthy glow boarding one of those planes. I imagine her in a short skirt and sandals, flying over my room, sailing across the sky beyond this glass window in this never-ending summer. From here, I watch the flashing lights of those airplanes pass by and carefully study each dot, each plane. I know that many kilometres in the distance, high up in the air, those dots all have little windows from which people with a life, who are going from one place to another, look back. I know that steam condenses in the little windows without transitioning through a liquid state, it turns from steam into ice, and that process is called sublimation. I touch the window with my hand and the glass here and the glass there become magnetised, bound by the desire for a better life. Suddenly, I think about the possibility of a mechanical failure abruptly changing the path of one of the 120 airplanes that take off from Barcelona every day, causing it to plummet right into the city centre. If an airplane crashed, it would immediately trigger a series of brutal tragedies, a mass of lives destroyed, something that seems impossible, something that defies this enormous and brilliant blue-black sky. That obsessive image of a falling airplane first comes into my head on this summer night and it will repeat in broad daylight, against the splendid indigo sky, several times a day. From then on, the brighter the sky, the greater my longing for the plane to nosedive, and I remember that once you and I took an airplane together and as it was taking off you held my hand to stop me from trembling but I realised that you were scared too.

XVIII. DEBORAH & SUSANNA

The omens were not good. A black crow had started to perch on my windowsill and when I awoke with aching bones I could sense its presence there, staring at me. Or perhaps it was something else, some other sign. Whatever it was, dear God, I'd felt it for days, the presence of something observing me, as if I wasn't alone in my house.

It didn't just happen at home. When I approached the neighbours chatting on the street to greet them, they'd immediately stop talking. Something was brewing and I wasn't part of it. Yes, Lord, I was being left out. Ever since Anne and Cotton started preaching your word to all the believers who wanted to listen, I'd gone back to being a simple businesswoman. Without the complicity of our project in common, all my planning had ended and all I had left was my old age. Having a plan keeps you alive, it gives you something akin to pleasure in the pit of your stomach. Making plans with Anne gave me the will to live, I felt like being in each other's company was eternal. But, now? Without the perspective of a new land to dream of together, to build our own society far from everyone else, I'd grown old quite suddenly.

Sure, go ahead and laugh about it. It must sound flippant, I won't deny it. But from one day to the next I started to notice how dry my hands had become, covered in spots, how wrinkled my knees. Me, who'd had the softest knees, as white as marble, which my husband had kissed and praised in those first few months when we still got along. Out of nowhere, the weight of my own body became too heavy for me, my hair looked like broom bristles, my eyes were bloodshot, I felt like perhaps someone had put a curse on me. Who was that old lady in the mirror? It couldn't be me, what had become of me? The worst part was feeling like I no longer had a future because I was nothing more than an old woman, one with more and more money, true enough, but old all the same.

I would wake up in the middle of the night to the black gaze of the crow and prepare a piping hot tea with apple jam for myself over the fire. Sometimes that extravagance alone would console me, along with knowing that my thoughts were still lucid, I had yet to lose my mind. Feeling the onset of madness would have been inconsolable in those downhearted days. That's all I needed, for the reverend or the governor to claim that I'd been possessed by the devil, and for them to wrench away the lands I'd finally been able to purchase, after all my sacrifice, after all that time.

On one of those nights I heard someone calling at my door, persistently, forcefully. Perhaps it's the crow, was the first thing I thought. And then, aware that would be impossible, I asked myself if perhaps I really wasn't going mad. It was when I opened the door and saw Anne, her hair dishevelled, her bonnet crooked and huge bags under her eyes, that I came back to my senses and acted according to instinct, as I'd done in the past. I showed her in and sat her down across from me at the wooden table where we'd sat so many times to talk.

She refused my offer of a hot drink and looked me directly in the eye. Anne, nervous as I'd never seen her before, not entirely out of her wits, only tired and tense as a wire.

'I need a favour,' she said. 'I know it's been a long time since we've talked. I know you've decided to stay on the fringe, but you're the only person I can trust for this. You have your reasons for not coming to the sermons – not that I share them, but it's what you've decided and I must respect that,' she smiled meekly.

'You know why I don't go, Anne.'

She interrupted me, 'I haven't deceived you, I never did. You just don't want to accept that the struggle is broader – we have to keep at it, whatever it takes…' Her voice rose louder and louder until I gestured for her to stop.

'There's no need.'

Anne smiled again.

We looked at each other until her smile bathed me entirely. Anne, my dear Anne. If I could only go back to one moment in my life, that would be the one. The chance to rekindle that sensation of joy revived me like a breath of fresh air. But it lasted only a second.

Then I realised Anne hadn't come alone. As dawn cast its light upon the room, I noticed hidden among her skirts was her daughter Susanna. Little Susanna, with hair the colour of coral.

'I want you to take care of Susanna for a while. I know you'll say that she'd be better off with a family, but I don't believe that. Susanna needs someone to guide her, to teach her all the important things she won't learn at school, and I don't have the time. I'm about to give birth again and I don't have time.'

Her voice faltered. It wasn't from the heartbreak of being separated from her young daughter, but simply from her accumulated exhaustion. By then Anne had twelve other children, one more on the way and a mission that was too important. What a paradox you laid out before us all, a real obstacle, a sick joke: how had we allowed our leader to become just another faithful follower who so clearly needed your help? At that moment nothing would have consoled Anne more than a voice that could inspire her – her own voice, but from someone else's mouth.

'Anne, you must rest. Promise me that you'll rest.'

But, was my voice enough, God? Was I enough for Anne? Would that day ever come again?

Her shoulders, which had slumped briefly, straightened again.

'Don't worry about me.' And staring off somewhere in the distance, beyond me, she added: 'We'll be able to do it, we must. I'm fine now, don't worry. Talking to you has lifted a burden off my chest. Or perhaps it is God, here, guiding me.'

We both smiled. And even so, the trepidation. And even so, we felt the distance between us.

'Come, Susanna,' ordered Anne with a calm, firm voice, the voice of a mother you can call on in need. 'You're going to stay with Missus Deborah for a few days, and I'll come back to see you when I can, all right?'

Susanna, with her enormous and clear eyes, nodded. I opened my arms and was once again hit by the scent of warmth and youthful perspiration, of fresh lemon leaves, of gentle life just beginning. When I opened my eyes again Anne had disappeared, closing the door behind her.

19. PASEO DE LA CASTELLANA, 11
(NOW)

That brings us up to speed, to the present. Once I had the money I left the city quickly, quickly, before I died, before I could kill myself. That's everything that has happened until now. Now, right now, in this precise instant, a dark turtledove crashes into the Plexiglas windowpane of my apartment. It happens a lot, especially when night falls, here in this fishbowl of a building, smack in the middle of a large avenue. There are fewer and fewer people who feed birds on the street. When dusk gathers, there are hardly any lights inside the buildings because this part of town is all offices. It's starting to get dark earlier, telling me that summer's far behind and we're finally diving deep into winter. The light in my apartment attracts birds as if they were moths, they're drawn instinctively, searching for heat. The windowpanes are kept so impeccably spotless that the poor birds can't see them, so they propel themselves forward without a second thought, like kamikazes. This has happened more times than the doorman can count, but that doesn't stop him from hanging signs in the elevators to notify the managers of the companies occupying the rest of the floors and the two lone neighbours who live inside this glass box. Every few days, workers come and hang from pulleys suspended from the rooftop to clean up the blood and the remains. Sometimes the birds also crash in the middle of the night. Thump, a sparrow. THUMP, a pigeon. You learn to distinguish them based on the sound of the blow.

I touch the bloody glass as the sky darkens. My hand doesn't get stained, of course. The blood is on the other side of this sealed chamber. My hand is clean. I go back to looking at the indigo sky that's not mine, this sky without mist, without salt, in which nothing moves. I feel the chill around me, the same one that's been disorienting me for months. And from here, as I watch the cars steadily drive by, I return to my litany. Which is this:

My sweetheart's girlfriend has eyes like a white rabbit: reddish, small and slightly bulging. I've studied her a lot on social media. My sweetheart's girlfriend is everything I am not: slim and nervous, with long marble-coloured arms and fairy-tale blond hair the shade of lemon sorbet. Sometimes I think of her pubis, it must be smooth and delicate like peach fuzz. I think of him entering her, slowly. Or of her mounting him, her narrow and youthful hips, riding him until she comes.

I don't know my sweetheart's girlfriend, but I think about her a lot. I've heard her voice through my computer screen because sometimes she appears next to him in interviews. They met through the Party, her job involves something technical and not especially interesting, but she – her whole aura – makes an impression on me. She explains timidly and with some difficulty what it's like to accompany him in his new post, assuming her secondary role. She doesn't have a gift for words, and I find her ineptitude even more moving. I would cradle her in my hands, like a soft little animal. At her side, he encourages her to speak, and I contemplate him and his transparent gaze, his protective instinct is so evident. I look at him: a renewed man, a freshly-shaven and coherent man who can convince everyone with clear and compelling phrases, and I understand perfectly what's happening. My sweetheart's girlfriend knows how to be loved, and she receives all that love like a warm bath, giving thanks with her eyes and her mouth as only youth can do. As only a new hopeful love can do. Hope is such a powerful parasite, it devours any doubt, destroys it with miniscule teeth, grinds it into smithereens and pulverises it until there's absolutely nothing left. They have hope and a new future, and that's why I know that my sweetheart's girlfriend will not complain or question anything because she feels like she deserves everything she's got, everything around her. She doesn't just feel it. She *knows* that she deserves it.

Trapped in my glass box, with the blood of the umpteenth turtledove still fresh, some of the fog in my head starts to dissipate. She knows she deserves it, unlike me. I never believed I was deserving of you, remember? I was a coward. I asked you time and time again. I was insatiable: do you love me? Do you love me? And you answered yes, yes, my love, yes, and I knew it wasn't true, that my fears were sinister, that you couldn't understand any of that. You don't know what it's like to be weak and cowardly. To be nothing but a shell of a person.

My sweetheart's girlfriend is, in essence, the opposite of me: I am resentful and delusional. I repeat this to myself night and day, this is me in my glass cube, this deformed experiment. Take a good look at me.

XIX. DEBORAH, SUSANNA & THE TREES

To say that Susanna saved my life may sound trite, but it's true, you know it. That's what happened: she saved my life. It took a few days for us to get to know one another, because she wasn't a quiet, easy-going child like Henry had been. She was restless. At first, she had trouble sleeping at night. When she did fall asleep, she would wake up screaming her mother's name. Even so, I soon found that she had a good and lively soul, and every morning she held me to certain routines which, after so much time, I had forgotten about. I got used to waking up together, preparing her breakfast, bathing her and taking her to school. Our routine became part of my newfound wisdom. I knew what I was doing, it pulsed through my veins and made me forget my own face and my entire past. Her youthfulness was like fresh hope for me, a blank canvas to fill, a reason to go on.

After dropping her off at school, I walked home silently in peace. I did my chores quickly and in an orderly fashion, with calm: I went to the market, managed my short-term investments – at my age that's all there was – and reviewed my accounts. I resolved everything within a few hours in the morning, before even putting something on the fire to warm my stomach. Susanna had given me order and words, a purpose.

As the afternoon unfolded and I saw her tiny body walking down the path, I felt the ease and joy of her company. I watched her walk uphill, alone, with her strawberry face. First nothing but a speck, then the size of a fingernail, getting bigger and bigger, more and more real, until she arrived and always cried out the same thing as she hurried through the door: 'Deborah, show me around your lands.' I was pleased to do so because I knew she had been a small and weak child, with arms and legs as frail as twigs, and she needed to be indulged with little joys, she needed to run around the countryside. So we went for walks in the fields, and she asked, every afternoon:

'Are these apple trees?'

'Yes, Susanna, those are apple trees. Their leaves are bright and shiny and their blossoms are pink, with a darker dab of pink in the middle. Remember them, so you'll be able to pick them out.'

'And the walnut trees? What colour are their flowers?'

'Walnut blooms don't have a special colour, silly. See them over there? The green catkins.'

'They look like fingers!' she shrieked, and her eyes got big and she broke into laughter.

'They look like fingers, yes,' I answered, and she continued her ritual of questions about fruits and flowers, and about the animals that visited our property at night. At first, she was scared of the sounds of the countryside, but soon my confidence in the land began to soothe her, this land of mine that was now hers, too. Neither the foxes nor the wild boars could harm her if she held my hand, her little hand in mine, and we would walk around until I told her: Susanna, it's time that you ate something.

And we would start our journey back home, and I would give her a large slice of hot bread with butter and honey to eat, and she would look at me with her curious eyes and raise her eyebrows and look at the bottle of wine, and if it was Sunday I would tell her: 'All right, but only one', and pour a bit of wine with honey into her cup, and fill my glass to the brim, and when Susanna drank her cheeks flushed, and they turned the colour of her hair, and we both laughed, 'wine strengthens the blood', I explained, and she nodded, feeling the same heat as I did in my cheeks and my chest, and we laughed and laughed until I said: enough Susanna, or Reverend Peter will hear us and think we've both gone mad, but Susanna just laughed louder, thrilled, unable to stop, until the room spun circles around her and I hoisted her up on one of my shoulders and put her to bed so she could rest for a while.

At first, when she woke up and everything was dark, I knew Susanna felt like her heart had been ripped out because she was thinking about her mother, and sometimes I could hear her crying, but that stopped soon enough. After a few days, Susanna awoke cheerfully and we would prepare dinner together, and she would tell me about what she had learned at school – readings from the Bible and not much more. So I taught her the letters of the alphabet and the numbers, always just before bed so they would stick in her head and she would dream of them. We studied the properties of plants during our afternoon walks, and learned about the stars on moonless nights so that no one would bother us. Her mother and I knew what a good education involved, and I had been entrusted to give one to her, so that's just what I was going to do. Nothing else mattered. Her mother had failed to come back, leaving us in that haven of peace.

It was on one of those afternoons, walking amongst the fruit trees, that Reverend Peter appeared with a sombre expression and told me: 'Deborah Moody, we must talk.' And I knew immediately that the time had come, something very serious had happened. Naturally, that crow on my windowsill was no coincidence, was it Lord? The time had come and I could taste the saltpetre and feel the sandy soil I feel right now, back then, at that moment, and I squeezed Susanna's hand and told her to go inside, saying I wouldn't be long.

20. PASEO DE LA CASTELLANA, 11 (NOW)

Tossing and turning.

I liked the streets of Barcelona, I think now. I liked the narrow streets of Barcelona because they could contain me. An alleyway, smelling of sardines and decay, eroded limestone, pools of piss and clumps of wet tobacco, beer cans, leftovers of uneaten kebab.

My memories there are of marble: the grey marble of the l'Abaceria market, the leftover bits of cod. Walking downhill through the city from that market to the Barrio Chino, I would sit down and wait for you at a bar I thought was 'authentic', the marble of Bar Almirall, a splendid, curvy bar that was smooth to the touch. Old marble gave me a sense of continuity. Old marble, not all those hipster vermouth bars. In my head, I revisit the spaces of my old loves. Bar del Centre, Almirall, Canigó, Sant Agustí. My cemetery of marble makes me feel alive, like a tourist of my own sweetness. Those idiotic loves I didn't save. Instead I embalmed them, like those crazy old Catalan ladies who have their tiny water dogs stuffed and say, 'Just look at little Terry. Isn't he handsome? Isn't he peaceful?' when in fact they've actually had the beast's canines pulled and their soul ripped out. C'mon girlfriend. You can do better than that!

I've been here in a glass fishbowl all this time and nobody's found me, so on the narrow streets of Barcelona I'll be able to blend in. I still don't know what my plan is, but it will come to me soon. I can feel it. I know it.

One day, like any other, I realise that it's spring in Madrid. The sky is indigo, cold and filled with grass and olive pollen, as the office workers smoke and drink their cafés con leche standing at the doorway. I watch them gesticulate from my window, they talk louder than usual, arguing, the men shift their weight from one foot to the other in their uncomfortable shoes, and they keep arguing, they string out their coffee break longer than usual. I decide to go down to the street for a walk and get my blood moving, perk myself up a bit. At the entrance to the building, right when I'm dodging the smoke from their cigarettes, I hear one of them say that the new mayor is a woman. 'She's a judge, man, a *judge*.' There's no doubt in my mind that you've won the elections as well.

That same night I dream that I go back. Back, so far back, my pallid hands, my veins filled with icy water, my childlike hands belong to someone else, but they're the same: I dream that I'm not saved by love and it doesn't matter. I dream of all the streets, like I do every night, until I get to a place that sometimes appears in my dreams, beyond Vallcarca, where the houses are white and the balconies have geraniums. Someone's there waiting for me. I feel them grab me by the hand and take me to a place with salty earth, there they trace a cross in the soil.

And I forget about her, about your current sweetheart with her round and stupid face. Round eyes, round mouth. I forget how she smiles and calls you darling, my love, she says, I forget, because someone's hand is holding mine and taking me with them. And I forget her blond hair and her round eyes like marbles, and I think you've forgiven me. I think perhaps it's the right thing to do, going back to you, going back to loving you, and how she's there, being three and one, and the salty water fills my mouth and tangles our hair and you love me, but the hand is pulling me toward the white houses with the geraniums, and the voice of a woman I don't know says: he doesn't hate you but he doesn't love you either. Is that what you wanted to know? Do what you have to. Prove what you're capable of. Either way, he'll never love you.

When I wake up the words echo in my ears. You don't love me so I can do whatever I want. You don't love me and I'm free. You don't love me and nothing I do will change that. And so, right at that very moment, I remember the dream and the image of the bridge in Vallcarca, and the exact plan is revealed to me, what it is I have to do. I *can* go back. In fact, I have to.

XX. DEBORAH: AN ANIMAL
FREEZES & THEN FLEES

Everyone knows that a blow to the flesh first leaves a reddish mark, which then turns purple, and eventually takes on the green and yellowish tones that indicate the bruise is fading. The blow itself lasts only an instant, true enough, but pain is a process.

Peter didn't mince words, something I was grateful for. Even so, his words knocked the wind out of me and I could hear only the crunching of dry leaves under our feet amidst the winter frost. I don't remember much. Just his pragmatic expression as we walked through my fields, and his words said with the haste of someone who knows something is being shattered.

They were going to arrest Anne for heresy. *Crack.* She'd disobeyed the laws of the colony, putting us all in danger. She'd created a division to favour her teachings of the Scriptures. *Crack.* Perhaps she'd had good intentions at first, but there was no doubt that she'd revealed a danger too great. It could cause instability in our entire structure: the relationship between grace and faith, that rift. Anne had weakened the structure, widening the fissure. It was now like a dam on the verge of exploding, an unmanageable deluge. If Anne had been preaching that spiritual intuition was the only way to have a relationship with God, then her beliefs foretold her demise. 'This is how it should be, Deborah.' *Crack-crack-crack.*

A blow to the flesh is sudden, there's no warning. That's why animals in the forest stop in their tracks: they fear the imminence of another blow. An animal is paralysed and waits to flee. Peter had spoken so I stayed still because I knew something had been set into motion; and the earth and sky were nothing but a spiral of matter looming over me. I was alone with my breath, I waited for Peter to break the ice, crunching like the bones of little dead birds, easily and without hesitation.

'They say that Hutchinson's youngest child is the spawn of Satan,' he whispered. 'Did you know that?'

I turned my gaze toward the house, with Susanna inside, and shook my head weakly.

'No, not the girl,' he said. 'The one who came after her, who was born deformed. Perhaps it's because of the company she holds. They say she and Cotton met long before they came here. Perhaps it was he who introduced these ideas into her head, who knows?'

I didn't move.

'In any case, I see no reason why anything should happen to you, Deborah. The problem started when men began attending her meetings, the promiscuous and filthy congregation of men and women who are not bound by marriage. Although I haven't heard – nor do I believe – that she's been unfaithful to her husband, but I suppose we'll never know. What sorrow! But we must remedy the gaping wound that woman has inflicted upon the church, the vast dishonour she's committed against Jesus Christ and the wickedness she has caused in so many souls.'

I know the reverend was watching me because I could feel his gaze upon mine, and the cold in my cheeks when he added:

'Don't worry, you should have nothing to fear. Your life abides by the righteous path, doesn't it, Deborah? At most you'll be called upon to testify in court.'

'Court?'

'Yes, the trial will start soon, but don't fret. Whatever you said at the women's meetings will not be used against you, as long as you can show your love for God, as you have up until now.'

Crack.

First an animal freezes.

When he paused I was able to look at his face.

'Your lands, Deborah, are the fruit of your labour and your honesty, are they not?'

'Yes, Reverend.'

'Prove it,' he said.

That's when I understood I was alone. You weren't there with me, dear Lord. All I had left was to run and run to my house and prepare a carriage and leave that very night, with only the clothes on my back, because you don't exist. Because we'd only been talking to ourselves, and in fact no one will save us.

First an animal freezes and then it flees.

21. CARRER DE PUIG D'OSSA (NOW)

From where I am now, the view is exceptional. I would never have believed that it could be so easy. The swallows, the dust-coated ivy, the deep, damp greyish tinge to the clouds all prove that summer is ending.

I've always associated bougainvillea with the Zona Alta. There isn't any bougainvillea below Bonanova, or at least not in my recollection. Bougainvillea, wisteria, buildings with exterior walls that have been painted and repainted in an ochre or salmon colour, time and time again, to cover up any possible imperfections. Striped school uniforms, women who carry themselves decisively in thick heels with their tanned calves and weekly manicures. Shops with French names, tea parlours, bridge clubs, thalassotherapy and refined oxygen spas, the more refined the better. And everything in solitude, isolated, very isolated. There's always at least four metres of distance between one person and another in this neighbourhood. Less than that would be unthinkable. I don't know why people insist on living in the city centre, in densely populated areas, getting together, sharing germs, bacteria, diseases. Longing for contact – that's for crazy people. Just getting into bed with a stranger could get you killed. Love is a monstrosity. Sex belongs to the underworld.

Now that I am who I am, I don't need to be coddled.

Over these last few days I've been able to confirm that rich people own nicer things simply because they are able to spend a smaller proportion of their income on buying nice stuff. It's that plain and simple.

Speaking of wealth: I can't stop thinking about how much cash I've got stashed in a suitcase under the bed. It makes me happy. It's at least enough to live here for ten years, more than enough. My landlady, Senyora Pilar, must like me because I rented this place for a song. I think she felt sympathetic when I told her I'm a widow, too. It doesn't bother me that she stops by every day. I like the company. A visitor who maintains her distance, strangely sororal, based on codes we both seem to understand. We don't need to feign proximity or take turns snivelling about our personal lives. She comes by for coffee when she can smell me grinding the beans, and always brings something along. A blueberry loaf cake, some cinnamon cookies. We sit down to enjoy the afternoon in silence, or comment on a flock of starlings, the changing colour of the leaves. All signs point to this being a good autumn.

The house is located beyond the Zona Alta, out where the city ceases to exist and the forest begins. That strange limbo dotted with scientific foundations, non-Catholic religious schools – Anglican, Adventist – and clearly illegal constructions built during Francoism and which nobody has dared to tear down. The neighbourhood is La Mercè, officially part of Pedralbes, although somewhat remote. Senyora Pilar lives in a white two-storey house on a street where mail is rarely delivered and the local bus passes many times a day but never stops.

Nobody will look for me here.

The weight has finally been lifted. I feel light, calm, at peace. It's as if all my cells have regenerated. I no longer have to think about anything. Naturally, I'm not taking the drugs any more, not even to sleep.

Yes, it's a miracle.

It was when I got here, where I am now, that everything settled down.

Like I told you, I'm a coward. Like I said, that's an important part of this story. So is your house. The one that was ours. Naturally, you didn't bother to change the lock – sure, I was depressed, but I didn't come off as the psycho I really am. You never thought I'd go back there without your consent. That's how men are: you're all convinced that people are going to follow the rules simply because you've been in charge of dictating them all this time, isn't that right? You treat us like trained dogs. It never occurred to you that the same dogs might chew up your clothes, pee where they're not supposed to and escape. That's right, escape.

The rules, oh yes, the rules. Aeons ago, when I was someone else, when I was with you, you made me follow one rule when it came to social media: don't show off how happy you are, it might awaken envy in people. I remember it echoing in my head. Don't be tacky, you used to say to me. Curiously, this wasn't a rule that applied to you, now was it? You've always done exactly what you wanted. And you haven't been entirely modest lately, have you? You know it. A trip to Greece with your sweetheart isn't modest. And now your life has been exposed, to me and to everyone else. Now *you* live in a glass box, and it's incredibly easy to follow your trail. 'A few days of rest,' you wrote beneath a picture of two plates piled with octopus and a turquoise sea in the background. 'ΥΓΕΙΑ.' Now, I can't help but laugh. Love is monstrous and also ridiculous. That's when I knew I had to go ahead and do it. I knew it was now or never.

It wasn't easy, but I finally figured out how to derail things. I thought a lot about you and me, about what we had shared, our streets and our past, and it turns out it was smack under my nose. All I had to do was exercise my own right to extractivism. I finally found a way to cash in on this city: by extracting something from this voracious animal that's made off with so much, you know? I found a way to achieve my political act. My final act. And it wasn't that difficult.

In fact, it was incredibly easy. Bleaching your hair at home is simple if you follow the instructions. The tone you get is the same shade as a blonde chicken, but it was useful for my purposes. Besides, I've transcended vanity. Beauty is no longer one of my objectives. I've also transcended my body. Grey leggings, a white visor cap, my hair in a ponytail. A little suitcase on wheels. I looked exactly how I'd intended, back in our old neighbourhood: like a tourist walking into a building where they've rented an apartment on Airbnb. I went entirely unnoticed.

I remember every step of the way. I'd rehearsed for so many months, from when I first devised the whole plan in spring until I was sure it would be failproof during the summer holidays.

I'll admit that I practically held my breath walking up those three flights of stairs. It had been so long since I'd been there, I could hardly believe it. Our home, the sacred scene of something that hadn't quite crystallised. Our home, that unborn child. I opened the door with my old keys, my heart racing, even though I hadn't taken any anxiolytics that day. I stopped taking them once I knew what I had to do. And now that all my senses were alive again, I felt so lucid that I could have recited, in one go, any of the laws forbidding me from being there. I was buoyant.

Our flat in Plaça de Jaume Sabartés still has the cement tiles. Even so, when I discovered that you'd changed the colour of the walls – you and her – to that pigeon-shit colour that's so 'in' right now, I was a little pissed, about that and the new furniture. I'm infuriated by your new status, your improved quality of life, the fact that she moved in bringing along her large oak table, the fact that her books and paintings are everywhere, artistically strewn about the floor. No trace of me, although, in all truth, why would there be? A new love interest, like I've already said, stings the most. Anyway, I collected myself quickly. I knew I had to keep my head about me, given what I was about to do. I opened the windows to air out the stuffy smell and the scent of aromatic candles she'd placed in every corner of the house. It stank like caramel.

I noticed that someone – which one of you was it? – had installed a decent watering system for the plants. The plants were going to be my alibi if some neighbour showed up out of the blue. Some busybody who heard the sound of footsteps or was puzzled by all the coming and going. I was going to be the well-intentioned friend who'd come by during the first week of August to lend a helping hand. Although that scenario seemed unlikely. There's no such thing as local neighbours in this city in August, and I was well aware there's no one left in the building who remembers us together. It's all tourist apartments now.

Let me tell you how it went. The best part. I sat down on the sofa, draped in an elegant white oriental cloth, and breathed deeply. One. Two. Three.

I've never been happier than I was at that moment. And I owe it all to you.

I showered quickly with cold water because the two of you were so prudent that you'd shut off the water heater. An icy stream in a silent, empty flat was like a baptism, and it helped me to clear my head and go over the plan. If my calculations were right the first ones would arrive in an hour, so I had to be quick.

I changed my clothes into an outfit that I'd brought along, chosen and paid for in cash at a neighbourhood boutique in Madrid. White blouse, dark skirt, mid heels. I brushed my hair and redid my ponytail. I carefully did my makeup using pearly eyeshadow and painting my lips light pink. The mirror reflected the face I was going for: a nondescript woman who no one will remember.

I took out my laptop and reread the notice to made sure it was spot on:

The false logo, the name, the text.

If you're looking for a spacious and luminous property in the heart of the Borne neighbourhood, near the Santa Caterina Market, this furnished apartment is perfect for you! It could be your new home. Bedroom with large balcony and street view. Open floor plan with integrated living room and kitchen. New on the market after recent renovations. Extremely well-lit, corner property. Large and sunny balcony. Entire flat decorated with an eye to detail and high-end appliances. The cement-tile floors, wooden beams and Climalit windows give this flat its quintessential 'Barcelona style', with characteristics of the Eixample neighbourhood, but located in the heart of the old quarter of town in one of the most coveted and fashionable neighbourhoods, with boutique shops and lively hip restaurants tucked away along its narrow streets. Located near Via Laitana, with good connections to metro lines (L4 Jaume I and L1 Arc de Triomf) and bus lines (bus stop for lines 19, 39, 40, 42, 45, 51, 55, 120, H14, H16, V15, V17). Just steps away from the market, surrounded by shops, services and entertainment.

The photos are from when we were thinking about doing that summer house exchange. Actually, the fact that the flat looks better now than it does in the pictures was a pleasant surprise. You invested in the place, renovating the kitchen and fixing the damp spots on the balcony. I imagine you, sweaty, on Sundays, saying to the blonde that there's no need to hire anyone because you're a real man, the type who carves wood and whitewashes walls. You can do it all, and that's great. That's wonderful.

When the first couple arrived, I was overcome by emotion. Two people who could have been us in the past, that same wishful thinking. Like two common thrushes in search of a nest, for whom the world is all too big. My eyes filled with tears. That's when the adrenaline started pumping through me, because I realised that my plan might actually succeed. What I was about to do was a work of art. One day you'll find out. One day you'll know the truth about who you really had by your side.

I explained to them, solicitously, that they could move in right away – but if they were *really* interested in the place, they ought to make an offer immediately. You should have seen me saying: 'I can't guarantee you anything, but since you're the first ones to see the place, I suppose you'll have a good chance.' Happening upon a flat for rent in Barcelona in the middle of August. You should have seen their excitement. Their little eyes. 'Yes, paying the deposit up front would help. Normally it's the first month's rent, along with the agency's commission plus VAT. Paying in cash would be faster, that way we'll stop showing the flat immediately. I'll give you a stamped receipt to prove the transaction is legal. Naturally, it will be deducted from your rent.'

The morning and afternoon went by without incident. Fifteen visits a day, for five days, from couples, friends, students accompanied by their parents and foreigners looking for a new life. It all added up to a pretty penny. I must confess that sleeping in your bed on the mound of cash, tucked into envelopes, was the best part. I let myself get a little carried away. But it was a lot of work, too. All the emails to answer. They all needed to hear the good news, and it had to be done right away. They were all so grateful. Every last one. Never had I experienced what it feels like to make people so happy, to deliver such joy. I was reminded of the beatific smiles on the faces of TV hosts when they make a phone call to present an award to some gullible or idiotic viewer. Now I understood that smile. It wasn't goodness, it was power. I liked having all that power.

I (or rather my pseudonym) was the one to give them the owner's contact details, meaning you. I told them all that I worked for you. All the emails were sent from your house, with the rental contract in your name.

Allow me to thank you for this image you've given me, without meaning to, and which I'll savour for the rest of my life. Allow me to enjoy imagining the telephone call, at some ungodly hour, to an idyllic Greek island, wrenching you from your haze of ouzo and unrushed morning sex while I'm riding in a taxi, holding onto a suitcase filled with money and dreams, heading north. You've given me the best gift in the world. The image will never abandon me. There are days when I relive that moment and I applaud, like a girl at the circus, enthusiastically. My only frustration is not being able to listen in on the call, or get a look at your dumfounded face when you find out what happened, when you finally figure it out. That is if you ever *do* figure it out, sucker.

Here, from my balcony near the Carretera de les Aigües Trail, I can see it all. If I strain my neck I can almost see your house, our house. A window is like a small shaft of light where an individual ecosystem flickers, the ins and outs of a pluricellular life. From here I can almost see the rugs, the books, smell the steam rising from a meal, from the day to day, hear the laughter of friends, all those things I'll never get back. And I'm glad. I don't want that any more. I'm in the best possible place. No one will look for me here.

Sure, I've thought about the possible repercussions if they do find me, but I'm not that worried about it. I don't think the Party would want it to come to light – after everything that's already happened and what's still to come. It's too dense and complicated to explain. Easy headlines work much better these days, especially with a party like yours. You people like slogans.

And me? I've learned to live like this. I've decided that I want to live like this. I know I've already got everything I need. My ascetism would be the same here or in a jail cell, I don't care. Besides, they won't catch me. What are they going to do? Search for my fingerprints? Who can you even trust these days? The Spanish national police? The Catalan regional police?

I don't care. None of it matters any more. You should know, like I do, that sooner or later history will judge us all. And you want to know the truth? I don't think things will turn out so bad for me.

There are days when I wake up with the dawn light and go out to the little front yard of my hideout, and the beauty of everything we've created, as humanity, takes my breath away. I've amassed so much power, me alone, that I can see and hear all the sounds on Earth. The sound of frost forming, an ant walking along a bit of moss, a chestnut ripening.

Sometimes my landlady comes up to my flat for a cup of coffee and she invites me down to the yard with her, to watch the sunset. She seems to understand what I need even before I do. That's when I realise the immensity of what we can achieve simply by stepping outside our zone of comfort. On those days, I sit in my little wicker chair and tell myself that, from here, all I have to do is wait – not for my punishment but rather for the thrill of the future still to come. When we're devastated by the massive flood, maybe I'll be saved and maybe I won't.

Who would have thought.

This sensation, this uncertainty, it's all I need to stay alive.

XXI. DEBORAH, THE CROSS &
THE SQUARE

So that's why I'm here, buried vertically. That's the reason behind this lifeless dialogue with you, dear Lord, surrounded by salt and mollusc dust. Back to the earth, I now belong here, after all the crossings.

Will-o'-the-wisps flickered on the night Susanna and I set off with all I'd saved up, leaving everything behind. The Indians let us pass because of Susanna's fire-coloured hair, like Regina Robinson's, which in their eyes had supernatural powers. I clung to her just as years before I'd clung to another safeguard by boarding a boat to flee from poverty. It didn't even cross my mind to take Henry along with me this time. He'd grown into a man by then, in Saugus. He had his own family, his own children, and no one would ever associate us. He was out of danger and it was up to me to save myself.

The first time I'd fled with my little boy of blond curls I'd done so without a plan, but this time my getaway found me with my own land purchased from the Dutch a few day's journey away. It was supposed to have been our new world, for all us women, guarantors of the spirit and life, our own Promised Land, with Anne at the helm.

Reverend Peter thought I'd been left in destitution, and that was enough punishment for an old lady, but in fact I was able to escape with something more. And to that end I had to make a pact. I learned that you can make a pact of silence with men if you behave as they do. That's why even the most honourable men close deals in bordellos: I'll keep quiet about your sins if you keep quiet about mine. That's the basis for everything.

I didn't attend either of Anne's trials, not the civil trial nor the ecclesiastical one, but her story made it beyond the Massachusetts border, all the way to where I'd settled. My new land was filled with water and salt, oyster dust and a flat horizon, where the sand swallowed up the sea. There I settled down with Susanna, after all the pacts. Once again I had a house, a child and a piece of earth. Once again, I started from scratch. I heard the news about Anne because as much as the reverend and the governors tried, the news leaked. Her trials were brief but heated. The transcriptions weren't made public right away, so it was only much later when I found out indirectly, through word of mouth. People spoke of her pale complexion and her birdlike hands, her deep voice as she answered all the governor's questions. Anne said that her body belonged to the colony, but that her soul belonged to God. Anne spoke her truth. They never discovered the girls hidden in the mountains, nor did I find out what happened to them. Perhaps they survived, although it's more likely they were discovered during the border disputes. Once again, all that bloodshed blurred together: blood as the result of sinful indiscretion mixed with the blood of war over lands. Everything culminated in the darkest of blood.

They tried to trap Anne in a scheme on the difference between faith and grace, but she was quick-witted and honest in her responses. She seemed not to understand that it didn't matter what she said: the problem was not in her words, it went deeper than that. It was her entire existence that had become intolerable. Anne defended herself as best she could, but she was accused of offending and disrupting the Church with her mistakes and revelations.

I imagine that Anne knew nothing could be done when it came to her youngest child. Until then, I thought Reverend Peter had just invented the problem to spread rumours, but at one of her trials Anne confirmed that her son had been born unhealthy. That's the story the farmers told me in our new settlement. Anne survived a dead child, but she was not beyond the final judgement. They say her last words to her old neighbours were a curse in the name of God, an attack on the rigid religious path that had recently begun in the Bay and which spread like a plague among its inhabitants. Her words were understood as proof of her heathen nature.

Beneath this soil I no longer feel the weight. I must remember what I knew back then: all parties must agree on their pacts. And we all know that to break a pact of silence there must be a traitor.

They accused her of summoning Satan, of being a pagan, and they used her sermons and her own fervour as evidence. Anne had chosen love. But, love to whom? It seems that Cotton had been sent to the dock but was never accused of anything. 'Men will betray you,' that healer had told me so many years ago. Anne and her family were ordered to leave the colony and settle somewhere beyond its limits, but Cotton received no sentence. A year after Anne had been banished, one of the servants told me that she and her younger children had sought shelter only a few miles from here, also near the sea, where ferns and azure irises grow. Cotton stayed in the Bay, became famous and prospered as a great authority of the colony. All he had to do was distance himself from her, as if their association had been nothing more than a bad spell, a dream from another era, and not an arm being ripped off, which is how Anne must have felt. The severing of an arm, her heart, her guts, and offering them up, with all her love, to her traitor. I cannot think of a crueller way to lose one's faith in God.

Some years later, I heard that Anne was having problems again. The burden of moving her family between different settlements meant she had ended up with practically nothing. Anne grew sick and dehydrated and could no longer provide for her clan. After she was banished, most of her supporters didn't dare make those long journeys on such dangerous routes. Indians lay in wait outside the borders of our New World, guarded by the Dutch. Only a few miles from home, Anne languished while I had everything: food, heat, prosperity and Susanna. Sometimes I could sense her proximity, Anne and her musty breath, prowling, howling like a she-wolf, appealing for clemency.

But a pact is a pact, and she who chooses love must pay for it. I didn't go to save Anne when the reverend came to warn me, nor did I do it later, when I could have offered her a hand. I had finally learned. I didn't tremble on the morning a grey turtledove perched on my windowsill, just another day, just another bird, an omen of the news that was to come. I got out of bed, nothing but sagging flesh, and prepared my black tea with the certainty that Anne had died that day. A turtledove at the window always announces misfortune, and that was the only possible tragedy. I later learned that the Siwanoy tribe had found her on their land and killed them all, including her children and the two servants who'd stayed with her. People say she had a silver cross in her hand, as a final offering to God, a shield to protect herself, but I was never able to confirm that tale. Property is property, and weapons are weapons. Anne, you fool, you were so occupied with saving the soul that you forgot the most basic precepts you'd taught me yourself. Flesh, blood, land. You fool.

That same day I got up, washed with cool water and went out on the grand esplanade in front of my house, my domains. I carried a metal object with a wooden handle, which the milky-eyed healer had given me so long ago, and with it I cut into the soil, like a butcher slices through the skin of a calf, with the same certainty. I used that cautery to trace the names of the streets in my town and went to the local authorities to give it a name: my town with two streets in the form of a cross and a square in the middle. This would be my land and my future. My property. I forgot all about the women and everything we'd built together. Everything fell away as if pulverised by the strength of salt and sandstone. Rest, at last. Peace, at last.

EPILOGUE: DEBORAH ON
PUIG D'OSSA STREET

I wasn't expecting you to concede me the gift of resur-
rection in the flesh. Perhaps, dear God, this is your last
sick joke. After all these years underground, waking up
in a bed was such an unexpected relief. Clean sheets, a
soft mattress, the scent of pines. It was something I could
never have foreseen.

My first day in this house was exhausting. I didn't
know this new life would turn out to be so easy for
me, that I would understand everything already. A new
language, a small but inviting abode where my bones
don't catch a chill and my skin doesn't suffer. I recognised, without ever having heard them before, the sound
of a coffeemaker, a mobile phone, a toaster. I knew how
to turn on the hot water tap, use a fluffy towel, switch on
a fan. Everything was new and old at the same time, and
therefore everything was both automatic and surprising.
Like the taste of blood when you lose a tooth; at first
it's terrifying but then becomes tremendously familiar. In
any case, it took a week before I dared to leave the house,
before I understood that I wasn't dreaming and this life
was real and I was here for a reason. Had you, perhaps,

dear God, finally delivered me to heaven? That would be impossible, by now we both know I'm not deserving of such grace.

When I opened the double-bolted lock of the door and walked outside it was an ordinary afternoon. I examined my surroundings. Gravel on the ground, a little garden of ivy and bougainvillea and a fence of red brick encircling a white two-storey house; beyond the gate, the cracked asphalt of the street. Puig d'Ossa street, I read, and then I understood. My home was on the ground floor and the upstairs apartment was empty. I walked down the street, mechanically, until I reached the square. The scent of pines and the damp breeze were somehow familiar to me. When I saw my reflection in the glass I noticed I was wearing a loose cotton dress and comfortable shoes. I'd also brought a shopping bag without thinking about it.

'*Pilar, què fas, maca? Feia dies que no et vèiem*,' a neighbour greeted me in Catalan, sitting on the porch of her house with two other ladies. 'Pilar, where are you off to, dear? We haven't seen you in days.'

'*Res, vaig a comprar peix i fruita, que m'he quedat sense res a la nevera*,' I responded. 'I'm just going to buy some fish and fruit, the fridge is empty, Opal.' Again the words floated from my mouth like soap bubbles. Like I'd felt so many years before, confident and spontaneous, as if launched by a catapult. Opal. I looked at the neighbours. I knew their names. Conxita, Montse. Why did I know their names? Why was everything so familiar?

You will make the crossing twice.

I walked a few blocks down to the greengrocer's. I felt the weight of the apples and was glad to see the first figs of the season had arrived. I bought both fruits, and knew how I would spend the afternoon: a fine sponge cake, warm and sweet, would give energy to us both.

I started back home and instinctively performed the tasks I'd resolved to do. I watered the geraniums and hosed down the white walls to remove some of the dust. Summer makes things dirty. Once I'd finished, I grabbed a little key hanging at the entrance, already sensing what it was for. Laboriously, I climbed the stairs to the upstairs flat and opened the door. The apartment had been shut for some time and needed to be aired out. I walked into the living room and opened the windows. From there, the view of the port city was remarkable. You could see all of Barcelona from that first floor. I knew it wouldn't be much longer until she arrived, I only had to wait.

The afternoon sun of this waning summer day had just begun to set when the doorbell rang. She had a blond ponytail, a suitcase I knew was filled with banknotes, and sparkling eyes. It wasn't fear that shined in her eyes, it was expectation. I knew that my angel had arrived, finally.

Come in, I said. This is your new home. She looked around, pleased.

It was then that I understood the memory of Anne would no longer torture me on moonless nights.

'It looks like a peaceful autumn awaits us, wouldn't you say?' I ask her now, wondering whether I should offer her some cake or wait for her to unpack her suitcase. Better to wait. We have all the time in the world.

AUTHOR'S NOTE

Despite the fact that Anne Hutchinson and Deborah Moody lived in Swampscott, on the outskirts of Salem, there is no documentation affirming they lived there at the same time. They were both expelled, this is true, by Reverend Hugh Peter. Hutchinson was condemned to leave the Massachusetts colony together with her family in 1638, while the archives date Moody's expulsion and excommunication in 1643. Eight of Anne's children, those who remained with her because they were still minors, were murdered together with her and her husband. Only Susanna was spared, because she was not present at the massacre. Although the dates do not match up, some oral histories were recorded at the end of the eighteenth century, the so-called 'Cautery Chronicles', in which a certain D. Dunch – Deborah Moody's maiden name – refers to a certain Anne H. However, English-speaking historians consider these texts to be apocryphal. There is clear documentation that after her expulsion, Moody settled in the southern part of Long Island, in New Netherland, and with the blessing of the director of the Dutch West India Company, Willem Kieft, she founded Gravesend, her own community, with religious tolerance and freedom of faith. Moody mapped out the streets of Gravesend in 1644. A copy of the original manuscript, showing the streets, can be consulted in the New York Public Library Rose Main Reading Room.

ACKNOWLEDGMENTS

This book would have been unimaginable without my early distinguished readers, Cristina Fallarás and Laura Fernández, who understood, when no one else did yet – not even myself – what I was trying to accomplish. Without them, the book wouldn't exist; my debt to them both is eternal.

To Isabel Ibiols, all my gratitude, for helping me feel like all this was easy when it actually wasn't.

Thanks to Isa Calderón for her understanding and encouragement.

And to Manu Tomillo for his patience, day after day.

TRANSLATOR'S NOTE

The scene is Barcelona in the early aughts. A group of female friends are cracking jokes about sex: 'We decide to go out for an aperitif on Escòcia street, and we fill up a bag with cans of beer. It's still daytime and we've no idea when we'll be back. We sit idly on a shady terrace. We order lots of food. Someone says she once *literally* had a shag between Pinto and Valdemoro, and the cackling kicks off again.'

I was right there, laughing along with them, until this very specific cultural reference about 'Pinto and Valdemoro' came up. Then I suddenly felt left out. Chapter nine of Lucía Lijtmaer's novel *Cautery,* I'm the translator and I missed this inside joke. Now what?

I lived in Barcelona in the early aughts. I was in my mid-twenties, like this group of women. I know all about those hot days that melt into warm evenings. I was always hanging around on the street somewhere with friends drinking cans of beer, almost broke but managing to scrounge up enough cash for some patatas bravas and fried calamari. I can imagine being part of this scene, cackling along to the ribaldry. But… what does it mean to have a shag between Pinto and Valdemoro? I don't recognise those as street names in Barcelona.

My research begins. I check Google: Pinto and Valdemoro are towns just south of Madrid, nowhere near Barcelona. I look up the expression 'to be between Pinto and Valdemoro' in Spanish – *estar entre Pinto y Valdemoro* – which seems to have multiple interpretations: 1) to express uncertainty when one doesn't know what will occur in the future; 2) to have to make a decision by choosing between two options; 3) to be waiting for a yes or no answer. It's like being in limbo.

So, where *did* this shag take place? What is the landscape like between Pinto and Valdemoro? And what are the origins of the expression? Legend has it that historically a stream ran between these two towns, a ribbon of water so thin you could straddle it and be simultaneously in both places at once. Today there's only concrete. In an online forum about the meaning of the expression someone quips: 'the only thing between Pinto and Valdemoro is the word *and*'. Another story relates that the monarchs used to travel from Madrid to Aranjuez to spend their summers at the royal palace, stopping overnight between these two towns, where the king visited a house of ill repute. Out of discretion, if someone asked after his whereabouts, the answer was vague: he's 'between Pinto and Valdemoro'. Yet another version of the story goes that the two towns were rivals and held a contest to ascertain which town made the best sweets; the king and queen were judges. After tasting both they were faced with a difficult choice and said, 'I'm between Pinto and Valdemoro'. Finally, the wine from Valdemoro was known as the best in the kingdom, whereas the wine from Pinto was not. To describe a wine that was neither good nor bad, it was said to be 'between Pinto and Valdemoro'.

Once I had gathered this background about the phrase, it became clear that the humour here lies in the fact that this popular expression is being used out of context, and the imagery of having a shag between these two towns (which most Spaniards have heard of but probably never visited) makes the joke work. Lijtmaer's use of the word 'literally' drives it home.

If I had stuck with a literal translation I would have lost some of the humour. Readers might have felt left out and confused, as I did, since the expression is too local for anyone outside of Spain to understand the reference. Instead, I chose to maintain Lijtmaer's format 'to be between X and Y', by using a well-known collo-quial expression in English 'to be between a rock and a hard place'. Even though this expression has a different meaning, *literally* having a shag between a rock and a hard place is a comical (although perhaps uncomfortable) image.

Literary translations are full of these conundrums – puns and plays on words – which I often choose to highlight on my first drafts, before coming up with a solution. These are the 'pickles' that stay in boldface, still in Spanish, for multiple read-throughs. They are my translator raison d'être, precisely because they make translation seem impossible at first. To solve problems like these I end up asking multiple colleagues and native speakers. I love having a reason to query random people who live around the world, from Madrid to Patagonia, Edinburgh to California, Berlin to Ecuador, where they perhaps work as an architect, lawyer or linguist. I relish drawing on these people, asking for their input, and then pondering my little word puzzles for weeks, working out possible solutions in my head as I go on a hike or swim laps or chop vegetables for soup. Since I started as a literary translator I have never really been able to leave my work at my desk until tomorrow: some pressing word game is always simmering in my mind.

When I look back at the pickles from my first draft of *Cautery*, the usual suspects are there: how to convey the distinction between addressing someone in Spanish's formal '*usted*' versus the informal '*tú*'? For example, I translated '*venga usted a merendar un día*' as 'Will you come to tea one day?'. By translating this as a question I felt more distance was created between the two characters, still strangers as their courting began.

In the previous chapter, the man being invited to tea had whispered a profanity into the woman's ear when they met in a stable: '*¿es usted de las que corre rápido, como los caballos?*' Just for fun, here's what Google translate came up with: 'Are you one of those that runs fast, like horses?' What machine translation fails to take into consideration is how the man coyly toys with the double meaning in the verb '*correr*', which in Spain means both 'to run' and 'to have an orgasm'. My version ended up less subtle than the original, but I wanted to make sure his crude inuendo came across: 'Are you the type of girl who runs fast and comes quickly, like the horses?'

Words with a double meaning pop up often; one of the most problematic Spanish words for me is the verb '*esperar*', which can mean both 'to wait' and 'to await' depending on context. Spanish writers love to exploit this ambiguity.

In chapter one, the readers are introduced to a catty and wry – possibly suicidal – woman as she envisions the whole city of Barcelona being flooded due to global warming. Instead of worrying, she proudly requests more plastic bags at the supermarket: 'I'm so desperate for us all to drown that I leave the lights on at home and I don't recycle', she boasts. Later, in chapter seventeen she continues: 'Besides, at this point I can only think about the brown flood rising to cover us all. [*Espero*], how much longer? It can't be too much longer now. No, it won't be much longer until it all ends.' We know she is in part eagerly awaiting the flood, gleefully looking forward to it – but here I chose the more ambiguous 'I wait, how much longer?' I even considered 'I can't wait'. It can be infuriating to have no right answer, and yet this is another reason I am drawn to literary translation. We have to make bold choices we can defend. I find this incredibly hard, but love the challenge.

Slowly, by the second or third draft these pickles get resolved, yet other macro issues emerge. My final draft requires me to read through the book at a faster pace, often in one sitting, whereupon the author's style must be consistent – her pacing, for example. Lijtmaer's sentences are often very long (and effortlessly so in Spanish), which helps her protagonists gain momentum. Their long-winded tirades are key to Lijtmaer's dark humour, dripping with irony or sarcasm. The best way to check whether her long sentences work in English is to read them out loud several times – and fall back on the beauty of punctuational pauses, such as the comma, semi-colon and hyphen.

Eventually I sent *Cautery* to my spot-on editor, Fionn Petch. With a keen eye, he weighed in on issues I'd overlooked in earlier drafts: reminding me to quote a translation of the Bible from the right time period (I ended up choosing the King James Version, originally published in 1611. I found that although the Geneva Bible from 1560 was often used in the colonies, Anne Hutchinson had been quoted using the KJV). We also discussed whether or not to use the historically accurate, yet now outdated and controversial, term 'Indian' when referring to indigenous people in the North American colonies. I thought twice about it, but all the texts written by settlers from that time period referred to the native and indigenous people as 'Indyans' or even 'savages'.

The examples above are just a glimpse into the heavily pondered choices and varied conversations that went into translating this playful book. I would like to thank my publishers at Charco Press for their patience and dedication, specifically Carolina Orloff for the opportunity (once we realised we were reading the book at the same time and loving it); and Fionn Petch for his detailed research on subjects as varied as autumn-blooming flower species and whether angels are sexed. I would also like to thank Lucía Lijtmaer for answering my multiple rounds of queries, her willingness to make slight changes to pull off her jokes in English, and also for reminding me that writing, as a process, is much more emotional than rational. Lastly, I'd like to thank my translator colleagues and native Spanish informants – there are too many of you to mention by name, but you know who you are. Thank you for your time, and for listening to me talk out my questions. I am forever grateful for all the solutions you've helped me come up with, as well as the instances where you set me straight when I took a stab in the wrong direction. What fun to play with words all day!

Maureen Shaughnessy
Bariloche, May 2024

C H A R C O P R E S S

Director & Editor: Carolina Orloff
Director: Samuel McDowell

www.charcopress.com

Cautery was printed on
80gsm Bookwove paper.

The text was designed using Bembo 11.5 and ITC Galliard.

Printed in December 2024 by TJ Books
Padstow, Cornwall, PL28 8RW using responsibly
sourced paper and environmentally-friendly adhesive.